STADDLECOMBE

Beth Kennington passionately wanted to pass her driving test, for one of the strange conditions imposed on the contenders for the Staddlecombe inheritance was a driving licence, as the late owner had been crippled by inexpert handling of a car. When Beth's cosy old instructor went sick, Adam Harcourt took his place and he didn't believe in cosseting his pupils. He was trying to lick the driving school into shape to please the boss, his fiancée's uncle. Beth, he was sure, would ruin everything.

STADDLECOMBE

Kay Winchester

FEB 1 5 1990

ATLANTIC LARGE PRINT
Chivers Press, Bath, England.
Curley Publishing, Inc.,
South Yarmouth, Mass., USA.

Library of Congress Cataloging-in-Publication Data

Winchester, Kay.
  Staddlecombe / Kay Winchester.
    p.   cm.—(Atlantic large print)
  ISBN 0–7927–0054–6 (lg. print)
  1. Large type books.   I. Title.
[PR6073.I476S7 1990]
823'.914—dc20   89–17011
                                                      CIP

British Library Cataloguing in Publication Data

Winchester, Kay *1913–*
  Staddlecombe.
  Rn: Emily Kathleen Walker   I. Title
  823'.914 [F]

  ISBN 0–7451–9630–6
  ISBN 0–7451–9642–X pbk

This Large Print edition is published by Chivers Press, England, and
Curley Publishing, Inc, U.S.A. 1990

Published by arrangement with the author

U.K. Hardback ISBN 0 7451 9630 6
U.K. Softback ISBN 0 7451 9642 X
U.S.A. Softback ISBN 0 7927 0054 6

STADDLECOMBE

CHAPTER ONE

Beth Kennington first met Adam Harcourt in the most unpropitious circumstances. It was a rainy day; wet as only a day in summer can be. Rain beat down so hard that it bounced up from the road, and windscreen wipers couldn't cope. Well, they hadn't coped with the weather on the van from the hospital. A new rule had been made that student nurses were not to cadge lifts from the supply vans, which was a pity. The laundry van was a plushy new one with handsome gadgets everywhere. So was the van from the grocer's and the florist's, so Beth had had to resort to the second-hand job run by the boilerman's nephew, because it was the only vehicle not specifically included in the New Rule handsomely printed and displayed wherever student nurses might be expected to take notice of it.

Beth had got rather wet because Will Grimsdale's nephew had not been able to afford to have the offside window replaced yet and as the van couldn't take Potter's Hill going up they had had to take the route past Staddlecombe, which was a mistake, because Beth couldn't resist getting out at the big wrought iron gates and wasting five precious minutes wistfully looking at the place and

1

getting all worked up about it as usual. Considering she was here for a driving lesson—her eighteenth—that wasn't exactly wise. But dear old Mr. Brown would forgive her and make allowances, she had thought comfortably. Mr. Brown was a dear. The kindest of driving instructors, and quite certain that she would pass her Test if she remembered all he had told her, and concentrated on things like her tendency to come up off the clutch too quickly, and to forget that such a thing as the mirror existed. And although Mr. Brown hadn't told her this, which was a pity, she also had a tendency to drive like an angel one week, and to bump off the clutch the following week so that he felt frankly sick by the time the lesson was over.

He thought perhaps it was his fault and that he was getting past it, so that when a certain event took place just after Beth's last (and rather unsatisfactory) lesson, Mr. Brown acknowledged the wisdom of his employers, and took what they called a Golden Handshake (which wasn't really very golden) and retired, looking forward at least to a little peace.

Perhaps, he thought wistfully, the man who would take his place, might be able to resist the appeal of Beth's blue eyes, beautiful in flashing anger as well as in limpid surprise that she and not the car, was responsible for what he was finding fault with. Perhaps the new man would be impervious to Beth's lovely voice, and her quite exceptional smile. Perhaps, too, the new man wouldn't even notice the comical set of her back when she walked, furious with herself mainly, away from the office of the Ace Driving School in Farmansworth High Street. Beth was a petite girl, but although she had small hands and feet, Mr. Brown knew her small build didn't stop her from being a very good student nurse, because he had heard what friends in Farmansworth General Hospital said about her, and he had seen her on the job when he had been a visitor there. He had specially tried to get a glimpse of her, to see if she was as inconsistent with her job as she was with her driving. He comforted himself that with time she would be just as good with a car as she undoubtedly was on the wards. The patients loved her, anyway, and he did, too, in a fatherly way.

If Beth knew that, she certainly had no such illusions about the man who was to take her dear Mr. Brown's place. He announced the change in circumstances before the receptionist could forewarn her. Poor Miss Hill, twittery as usual, had got as far as saying, 'Oh, Mr. Harcourt, this is your next pupil—' when the most good-looking young man Beth had yet seen, marched across to her little book of appointments she was putting

3

on the counter, picked it up before Miss Hill could reach it, briskly counted the lessons, and said, 'Seventeen already. Ah, then I imagine you will be capable of driving away from here, or would you like to be driven to the "nursery" streets?'

Not a good beginning. Miss Hill shook her head in despair as she watched Beth's pretty legs working overtime to keep up with Adam Harcourt's long easy stride. There would be sparks flying in Car No. 3 this morning, she feared.

Farmansworth had been an attractive market town at one time. Beth and her family had moved here after the alterations had started to take place, so that she was still confused with roads that had been sealed off, and new buildings replacing comfortable old ones. A fly-over had diverted all the traffic, so that although her hospital was in view, it was a very long walk by way of back streets to get to it.

Beth wondered, as she drove through the narrow pass between parked cars, if Staddlecombe itself would one day be incorporated in the reaching tenacles of a growing town, and swallowed up. What had old Mr. Unwin thought, when he had made that impossible Will, setting out such difficult conditions?

A cold voice beside her said, 'Turn left at the next junction,' and Beth jumped, her foot

4

coming up from the clutch and stalling the engine. Old Mr. Brown, with his cosy voice and calm manner, usually said to her, 'Now then, little Nurse Kennington, let us resolve to do our best today. Settle down now, and let me have Cockpit Routine, please.' He had always said please, and Beth always said parrot-like, as she did the actions: 'Door closed (is your door closed too?) and seat adjusted. Seat belt on. Mirror, gear in neutral, hand brake on. Yes, all okay,' although sometimes she forgot something, such as the gear handle, and he would hold the ignition key high out of reach until she remembered, and he would shake his head and chuckle and say, 'Never mind, we'll get you through that Test somehow, first go.'

He really had been such a kind and patient man, and that could hardly be said for the gentleman on her left, she thought furiously, as he sat back with a weary sigh, and raised fine grey eyes to heaven in a frustrated gesture that was guaranteed to put anyone off. She wrestled with the gears, clutch, any pedal within reach, well aware that all of the drivers held up behind her were going to put impatient thumbs on horn buttons any minute now, because the road was too narrow to pass her. Finally she persuaded the engine to re-start, and the roar made an angry bark from the left of her, 'Foot off that gas pedal!' and from then on, things went from bad to worse. You would think that the car was made of frail porcelain, she thought, the way this man beside her begged her in sharp angry tones, to keep off the foot brake pedal, not to roar the gas and not to jam the gears, to be gentle with the clutch, and to keep looking in the mirror and to watch her speed. When he shouted, 'Your feet! Watch your feet!' and she misguidedly looked down, he took over the dual controls and steered her to the side of a road that miraculously had little or no traffic in it, and begged her to put the gears in neutral and turn off the ignition.

'Now, look at me!' he commanded.

She hadn't really had a good look at him yet. He really was too good-looking for words. Roll her three favourite film stars into one, taking the best points of each, including a cultured and quite musical and deep voice, and that was Adam Harcourt. And didn't he know how handsome he was, Beth thought angrily.

He added insult to injury by asking, quietly and reasonably, 'Why are you taking driving lessons, Miss Kennington?'

She gasped. It was like cold water over her. 'Because I want to. I need to,' she said.

'Why? I need to know,' he explained kindly.

I won't be intimidated by his six foot three nor his broad shoulders, she promised herself. And if he demonstrates what a wonderful driver he is, I simply won't care. She drew a deep breath and said, 'Every nurse should learn to drive. If I get through to my Finals—'

'Ah,' he interjected, meaningfully.

'—I shall need a car because I mean to go on the District,' she snapped, with heightened colour. How dared he? Nobody had ever suggested that her work at the hospital wasn't good, and she didn't intend to let this man undermine her confidence with her work, even though he might well convince her that she would never make a good driver.

Surprisingly, he allowed, 'That's a good enough reason. But whoever has tried to teach you, has been going about it the wrong way!' That, to him, was as obvious as the day. He was surprised at the amount of indignation that was called up in Beth's flashing blue eyes. Her soft full mouth trembled with all the things she would have liked to say to him, but she was also aware that her rather expensive lesson time was fleeting. 'Well, you try,' she invited.

'I will. I intend to,' he said blandly. 'From the very beginning. So kindly get out and take my seat, and I will drive you to the nursery streets for a little practice on the first lesson.'

'Oh, no!' Beth exclaimed, really alarmed. 'I couldn't.'

7

'Come now, you can't mean you need a chaperone,' he taunted.

'Don't be silly, I'm a nurse! I meant that I couldn't because I haven't the time. My Test is coming up soon and I just can't afford money for more lessons if we waste this going over early ground.'

He raised his well marked dark brows very high indeed, so that there was really no need for him to say anything, but he did. He pointed out, quite succinctly, that if she didn't take his advice she would fail her forthcoming Test as sure as night followed day.

Beth silently changed seats with him, and spent the rest of the lesson time seething over the controls, and doing a silly little exercise of creeping forward at snail's pace and stopping when he rapped on the dashboard. He intimated that until she could do it as slowly as he wished and stop without stalling the engine, there was really no point in her doing anything else.

He drove her back to the office at last, in such a boiling fury that she had to force herself to say a civil goodbye to him when she left.

★　　★　　★

Beth was a favourite everywhere except at the driving school. She was on the Women's

8

Surgical Ward, and all the patients gave her advice from their male relatives, although as most of them drove lorries or buses it wasn't much help. Only gentle Rose Carver, the infant school teacher who lived alone with her aunt in a small cottage in Pockling Parva, could help. Rose drove a car and so did her aunt when her rheumatism didn't trouble her, and because Rose missed the school and its work so much, she persuaded Beth to bring her Highway Code and Rose went over it with her whenever they could. 'But your half brother Don should help you with practice, as he's in a Service Station and sure to be a good driver. You really do need plenty of practice,' Rose said.

The others agreed, though they promised to persuade their men folk to tell Beth when they visited, how they had learned to drive, even though Mrs. Gibb's husband was on an all night lorry and Mrs. Tally's son was in charge of the laundry van.

Mrs. Arky was sure her husband could give Beth a few tips about how to reverse round a corner. 'You should just see my Joe back his removal van into a little narrow opening, duck; takes your breath away to watch him. I won't look, but he says it's easy when you know how!'

Easy when you know how, Beth fumed, and wondered why dear Mr. Brown hadn't told her he was going to leave. Surely he

9

hadn't been upset with Beth's driving? He wasn't young, of course, but he had always been so calm, so patient and comforting.

One of Beth's two great friends, Frances Loxton, who had started to train the same day as Beth, and had so many freckles on her face that there was hardly room for a pin point between them, assured Beth that her elder brother had said there was nothing in driving. But Grace Peters, who had known Frances since they had been in junior school, said scathingly, 'Have a heart! Your brother was in and out of the cars since he was a nipper. He's more or less absorbed it like playing with toy guns and learning to swim.' Grace could be scathing at times, but she had the makings of a good nurse, and the girls made a trio that blended perfectly. Perhaps because Beth was the undemanding one, the one who was more often thinking about her steady boy-friend and writing letters to him, leaving the other two as a close pair.

Beth, making beds and doing the B.P. round, thought about Howard often. He loved her, he often said so. He told her it was good for a nurse to be going steady with an up-and-coming solicitor instead of a doctor. He told her everyone knew Howard Quested and his family, and that was good for a nurse as well. But did she love him, Beth often fretted. And why didn't he ask her if she did?

But that particular week, Howard's father

10

had gone to the States, and his grandfather—still coming to the office for half of each day—had gone to Scotland to see a very old client who was ill, so most of the work fell on Howard.

Beth thought of him, sitting at his father's desk; a thin young man with an unsmiling clean shaven face and such heavy frames to his glasses that they made his face look more frail. She realised that Howard was neither as tall nor as heavily built as the odious Adam Harcourt, nor was Howard's driving so smooth and perfect. Howard was anxious and earnest and really rather a dear. He never snapped at her nor was he rude, like Adam Harcourt. Adam Harcourt was cropping up as a comparison with too many people she met, she scolded herself, and really, he didn't merit it. She hardly knew the man. But, she thought in surprise, she was thinking about him all the time now, although it was only an hour's lesson once a week.

This was Beth's day for meeting her mother, who came over by bus from Larkbridge and told Beth all the family news. It was odd, Beth reflected, how she was still so lost if her mother didn't come over, and yet the news from home always stirred her up, spoilt the placid existence she had enjoyed at the hospital until Adam Harcourt had come into her life.

They met in one of the many restaurants in

11

Farmansworth, and had tea and scones, and then Beth left her mother to go round the shops or to the pictures. Beth's mother's weekly treat.

She was still a handsome woman, Beth thought, as she watched Lydia Whiterod get off the bus. Widowed three times, Lydia was the sort of woman who fiercely preserved her youth, but needed to have attention and affection poured on her. Beth supposed her three husbands had spoiled her for the buffeting of family life. Lydia was certainly not the comfortable sort of Mum one ran to with one's troubles, as Grace's mother seemed to be. One felt one ought to cosset Lydia, Beth thought, with a wry smile, as she went forward to meet her.

'Beth, darling!' Lydia said, putting her cheek briefly against her daughter's soft round one. 'You haven't got any make-up on! What can you be thinking of? Oh, well, I don't suppose they allow it at your hospital. Oh, and you've come out in your uniform, too. No time to change, I suppose. Never mind, let's find some tea. I'm dying for a cup, and I've lots to tell you!'

Beth reflected that it was as well that her driving lessons hadn't needed to be discussed. Her mother wouldn't want to hear about *them*. Lydia said, as she successfully found a table in the window of the Blue Tea-Rooms, and looked out appreciatively over the High

Street with its busy afternoon shopping scene, 'You are a lucky girl, working in a town like this. You don't know how dreary it is in Larkbridge. I can't think why we ever went to live there!'

A waitress came and Lydia ordered tea, and patted her dark hair into place, briefly glancing at Beth's unruly short cut escaping from under her nurse's cap. Beth thought wryly that that last remark wasn't really answerable. The reason was that Lydia's first husband had inherited the house there; the second husband hadn't happened to have a home and half the family were already ensconced there, and by the time Lydia's third husband had arrived, there was no question of moving. Everyone was deep-rooted in the Victorian terrace house, the whole three floors being just big enough to take them all, counting poor Len Whiterod, who had rented a room there, on his return from a stint abroad, and he had never got round to thinking of making a change, after marrying Lydia.

Lydia collected family from her husbands. Don, it was true, was her own son by her first husband, but then Don Jeffers senior also left behind the infant daughter of his own sister. It was of Isabel Robins that Lydia clearly wanted to talk to Beth.

'You know, Beth, she's a dear girl,' Lydia started earnestly, her chin in one hand, elbow

13

on the table, fixing Beth with her eye. '*But* . . .' Here it came, Beth thought. '*But* . . . well, the truth is, she and Shirley just don't get on. Shirley's so serious, so . . . well, she is apt to be a little possessive about her things and poor Isabel is just the reverse. You know, Isabel would lend the clothes off her back if any one wanted them . . .'

Lydia paused, coloured faintly, and hurried on, 'But of course she never has anything worth lending, and she always wants to borrow Shirley's things. *I* know that! You don't have to look so reproachful. And I know Shirley being a teacher at the local primary school, does have a lot on her mind, though I do think that just one little boy being tiresome . . .'

'Mother, if you're referring to the Imberholt boy,' Beth broke in, striving to be fair, 'I've seen him. He's bigger than the others and he can make a riot at the drop of a hat, because the other children are scared of him. Shirley ought to leave there if she can't manage. I think they ought to have a male teacher.'

Lydia gasped in horror. 'Don't let Shirley hear you say that! She regards it as a challenge. She won't give up that job of hers, not for anything.'

'Then what is it you're saying to me?' Beth said gently.

'I want you to suggest a solution, only not

14

that one! We've heard that one before and agreed it won't do,' Lydia said quickly. 'And it won't do to suggest that poor Isabel goes to live elsewhere because she can't afford other digs. Besides, it isn't only that.'

Beth thought quickly. What else could it be? 'Don isn't in any trouble, is he, Mother?'

'There you go! Whenever I'm a little worried . . .' She broke off as the waitress brought their tray of tea-things. When they were alone again, she said, having marshalled her thoughts on another track, 'It isn't just the girls. Oh, I know you think that the step-daughter of one of my marriages, and a niece of another of my husbands, have no claim on me, but just wait until you marry. You'll see where your loyalties go.'

Beth thought of marriage. Howard in his precise way had never presented himself to Beth's imagination as a husband, a father of young children. In her thoughts he never got further than the young man working up to choosing a very conventional engagement ring. The man in her thoughts now, rampaging down to breakfast, late for his office, was not Howard, but Adam Harcourt, saying coldly, 'Do you not think you could have good hot coffee ready just for once, and do you have to burn the toast?' She went scarlet. She just stopped herself from visualising him on the floor with two small boys riding his back, whipping him and

15

yelling, because she couldn't imagine him grinning widely up at small children.

Her mother said, 'Now why are you looking embarrassed? You really are a funny girl. There's nothing wrong with speaking of one's husbands, even if they are no longer with one, and I'm sure I can't think why these gentlemen should have wanted to marry me when some women can't even get one,' and she broke off, biting her lip, for Isabel's main grouch in life was that her boy-friends always faded away before anything serious had developed. 'As I was saying to Ewart only this morning . . .'

Ah, now here it came, Beth thought, wondering why she hadn't anticipated this before. Ewart Nettlefold, her mother's brother who worked in a local bank and was always worried because he couldn't balance his cash as fast as the younger clerks.

'Poor Ewart's health isn't as good as it was. He really ought not to stay in this country. A branch of his bank in mid-France, I always tell him, would suit him very well.'

'He can't speak French,' Beth pointed out helpfully, because she knew what was coming.

'What about your driving lessons, dear? Until you pass your Driving Test you won't stand a chance in that rat-race, you know. Now don't look shocked. It kills me with anxiety, thinking of how hard you must be working to take your Test, but you know very well there is a time limit, and three more people standing to inherit in your place if you don't pass the conditions test.'

'We all stand a chance, Mother, whoever the other three people may be,' Beth said patiently. Ever since crippled old Mr. Unwin had died, people had speculated about this unusual Will of his.

'Ah, that's another thing I wanted to speak to you about,' her mother broke in quickly. 'I'm glad you reminded me. We simply must find out those other people's names, and your Howard is just the man to do that! Well, he's a solicitor, and you're not going to tell me solicitors don't hang together and talk these things over, and he could find out for you, that's if he doesn't know already. It would be just like him to keep mum about something so important to this family.'

Beth shook her head. 'No, Mother, not to the family. To me,' she said.

Her mother took seconds to take that in, and then her jaw dropped. 'You can't mean that, Beth! Oh, no, I won't believe that you meant to say that! I mean, all that money, and not for your own family! No, that isn't you!'

'The old gentleman wanted whoever got the money in the end to put it to furthering a career, not bailing out lame duck relatives from trouble, and well you know it, Mother. Besides, they aren't my relatives—well,

17

perhaps Don, but that's all. Oh, and Uncle Ewart, as he's your brother. But they're older than me. I don't have to carry them on my back for life. Besides, it isn't right to live on the expectation of something that may never happen.'

'Oh, is that what you really mean?' Her mother's face cleared. She was thirty-nine, she always said. Elementary arithmetic made her at least forty-one, when you came to consider Don's age. But the years had dealt kindly with Lydia, Beth thought, and she didn't know why she had said that to her mother, because it had always been settled in her mind that if she ever got that money from the old man's estate, she would leave the hospital and take all of her family to the sunshine for a month or two, and then set about finding each of them something—either a career or marriage partner. But the cool assumption on their part that she would take them under her wing nettled her.

'Yes, that's what I mean,' Beth said, gathering up her things. 'And the way my driving's going, I shall never pass my Test, because there's always something I do wrong, and now Mr. Brown's left . . .'

Unwise, she told herself furiously. Her mother pounced on that admission. 'Oh? That old man has left? Well, and about time. I saw you in the car with him one day and he looked half asleep. I hope you've got a younger man teaching you. I think I'll go along to the Ace driving school and have a word with them. If they know the reason why you're taking the Test . . .'

'No, Mother!' Beth's sharp young voice silenced Lydia, who sat and gaped at her. 'If you do any such thing, I shall know, and if and when I do get that money not a penny will any of you see. Now I mean that. I get through my Test under my own steam and don't you go near there. Understood?'

Her mother dropped her eyes, and while she was saying quietly, 'Of course, dear. I don't know what made me say I'd go along and see them! I won't have time and anyway, what a boring thing to have to do!' she was secretly thinking, little Beth's in love. Now who with? Hardly likely that there was anyone worth considering at the driving school. Certainly not that dreary young solicitor that Beth had been going steady with for some time? That left either one of the doctors—and Lydia didn't think that was likely—or a patient. A rich young patient, that was it. Lydia decided that she would forget about visiting the driving school and take on, instead, a self-imposed visit every so often to the hospital where her daughter Beth worked.

CHAPTER TWO

Adam Harcourt had had a bad day at the driving school. He asked himself again why he had let himself be talked into leaving his original job to take on teaching people to drive. Coraleen had persuaded him, of course, because her uncle (so she said) had a pressing need of good young drivers. He frowned. Why did he let Coraleen persuade him to do so many things he didn't want to do?

He was dining at Coraleen's home that evening. He wished he wasn't. He wasn't in tune with Coraleen these days. But it was necessary to attend tonight, anyway. Her uncle was his immediate boss, and it was policy not to annoy him.

As Adam drove up the drive of the white stone house that Oliver Mason had not long purchased, he wondered what life would be like for him in the future. He asked himself how he had got into this situation. He had been on the staff of the engineering complex also owned by Oliver Mason, when Coraleen had returned from a holiday in Europe and had dropped all her belongings as she was getting out of her car. Adam had been crossing from one block to another at the time and stopped to help her pick them up.

He frowned. He didn't remember much else about that first meeting, yet it had resulted in his getting engaged to her. She was good-looking, well-groomed, witty, but then so were several girls he knew. He supposed it was her trick of seeking him out to ask his advice about things that had been rather appealing. She had asked him to teach her better driving.

Those lessons hadn't really been necessary. She invited him to parties at her uncle's house, and got him invited to the houses of her friends, and he had found himself either as one of a party, or Coraleen's own escort. There had been concerts: he had to admit that he couldn't resist pianoforte recitals, and it was nicer to go along with someone than to go everywhere alone. And there had been no reason why he shouldn't have gone around with Coraleen.

But things hadn't stayed there. He had since discovered that with Coraleen, things always moved on a little, and usually the direction she needed, was the direction that everyone else took. For such an apparently sophisticated, pleasure-loving girl, she had a rather devious mind, he thought, frowning. And this was the girl he allowed to turn his footsteps into the driving school. He recalled the way Coraleen had put it: it was one of those small odd ventures her uncle went into, found it was a lame duck and needed

21

someone to brisk it up for him before he sold it off his hands. Would Adam be a dear and help out, as he drove so well?

Coraleen was the girl who had somehow become engaged to him. That had been at the end of a noisy and particularly irritating party, when they had left before the others, and somehow he had found himself agreeing with her that life might be more peaceful for both of them if they were to get engaged. And then very soon after that, he heard that he had something cropping up in his own life that might have made everything so much more interesting . . . old Maurice Unwin had died, and he was one of the four people mentioned as competitive beneficiaries under the very odd Will the old man had made.

Coraleen hadn't been too much interested at first, but now she was. She wanted to know who the others were, and had quarrelled with him when he had forbidden her to try to find out.

One day she would discover that he had been distantly related to the old man. Adam hoped that Coraleen wouldn't discover other things about him, but he supposed glumly that she would probe and pry until she knew every little precious thing he wanted to keep to himself. But should one try to keep things from the girl one was to marry?

He was still frowning about that when he drove the car round to the garages. Vic

Imberholt was there. Imberholt and his wife ran the place. They had a most trying small boy. Adam wondered why there had to be a married couple with a child at all. He was only too thankful that he was allowed to run his car into a separate small garage and to lock the door on it.

There were two other visitors there tonight. A man who was closely engaged with Oliver Mason in business, and the young solicitor in whom Mason had suddenly become interested: Howard Quested.

Oliver Mason had discovered another small driving school in the next town that he wanted to buy and merge with the Ace Driving School he now owned. The talk during the meal was depressingly like an extension of the day's work, Adam thought with some surprise. At his old job, before he had met Coraleen, he had enjoyed talking shop after work. But driving was not a thing to work at, not when it involved beginners who slammed the gears and maltreated good new cars.

Oliver had great ideas for the Star Driving School. 'Why the Star?' Adam wanted to know, idly, and Oliver, tall and portly and highly coloured from his love of his brandy after dinner, said with a fat chuckle, 'On account of it being in the back yard of the Star and Garter Hotel, of course. Though I don't mind telling you Adam, my boy, that

I'd rather have it re-named the Garter Driving School. A little more plushy, eh? Suggesting the Order of the Garter, what?'

Coraleen said coldly, 'I don't like it, Uncle. People might think it's some other kind of garter. Why don't you re-name it the Ace, if you're going to buy it? Have it as another branch of the one you have here?'

He glowered. He didn't like to have his ideas pushed aside. 'I'm not sure I'm going to keep that one yet.'

Adam raised his head in sharp surprise. 'How is that, sir?'

'Nothing to do with you, my boy. You've only been in the place a couple of weeks. No, there aren't many pupils and they don't get through their Driving Tests. Well, name the pupils you have, and tell me, if you can, what good they'll be! From what I hear they're not likely to do us much good.'

'Adam has all girls, and they make him very bad-tempered,' Coraleen said teasingly. 'He also gets hefty dustmen who practically wrench the steering out, and foreign students who don't understand what he's saying.'

Adam frowned at her but his uncle insisted on hearing about the pupils.

Adam told him about the male pupils and their chances but Coraleen wasn't going to let him get away with that. 'What about the elderly typist from the shoe shop?' and Adam, much harassed by that fluffy elderly lady and her bad performance, snapped that he'd get her through her Test somehow, some time.

'Not good enough, my boy. I want to build up a reputation for pushing them through their Test first time, otherwise it's not much good limping along with the same poor reputation that any little one-man driving school may have.'

Adam said coldly. 'Some of the younger people may get through first time. I don't know. There aren't any pupils that I started with. I have to iron out the things the previous instructor let them get away with.'

'Cosy old Mr. Brown,' Coraleen said, hugely enjoying herself. It was a long time since Adam had let her needle him like this.

'I suppose you're getting at Miss Kennington,' he snapped.

Howard's head shot up at that, but they weren't looking at him but at Adam and Coraleen.

'Well, among the rest of the comical ones, yes,' Coraleen allowed. 'I drove behind your car last week, and my heart was in my mouth many times at the things you let her get away with, or had she got you so petrified that you weren't able to use your dual controls?'

'Now listen,' Adam protested, as he noticed his employer was looking far from pleased. 'You shouldn't drive behind me, Coraleen, you know better than that.

Anyway, Miss Kennington drives well enough sometimes. It's just that she's erratic . . .'

'That wasn't what you said last time, darling,' Coraleen chuckled, and to her uncle and the others, she explained: 'He came in looking as if he were going to burst and he said if that stupid Kennington girl didn't go less mad at the controls next week he'd knock her head against the school wall to see if he could . . .'

Adam's angry eyes were lost on her. It was Howard's face that made her stop in mid-flight. Howard said icily, into the silence, 'Are you by any chance referring to Nurse Elizabeth Kennington at the Farmansworth General Hospital? That happens to be the lady I am going to marry.'

★   ★   ★

Not a happy evening. Coraleen insisted on walking out to the garages to say goodnight to Adam, undeterred by his frosty manner.

'Well, it was his fault, darling, for not mentioning it before we got too far. He could have. Her name was mentioned earlier. Anyway, what does it matter? He daren't kick up. His little firm wants Uncle's business too badly. He knows they'll get the rest of Uncle's companies in time, if they behave themselves.'

'You talk of them, and everyone else employed by your uncle, as so many puppets on strings,' Adam said, not enthralled by the big business that had been discussed that night.

'Well, you don't have to stay a puppet all your life. As my husband, you'd be one of the people pulling the strings,' she said lazily. 'And what do you care about that silly little Kennington girl? She's getting the husband she deserves: the dreariest most inept young man I have ever seen in my life.'

Adam might have had something to say about that, too, for whatever else he had found Howard, dreary also, he had not found him inept. He was good at his job. Adam, who was proud of whatever he himself undertook, recognised the pride in the young solicitor's bearing, realised he would do well enough. The dreary manner probably arose from lack of experience. He'd be all right at his job, Adam felt, when he's been doing it another five years. He didn't like Coraleen talking like that.

He was about to say so, when he noticed that the door of the garage had been forced. He hurried over to it and found a shadowy form with a torch, peering into his car.

'What the—' he began but the form straightened up and he recognised Vic Imberholt.

'It's only me, sir. Didn't want to alarm

27

anyone until I found if any damage had been done to your car. There hasn't. Sorry about this, though. Must have been village kids—stay up late, they do. I just happened to get here in time to scare 'em off. I was looking at your tyres and petrol cap, but it's all O.K.'

Coraleen wandered in behind Adam and said lazily, 'What fuss! It was probably your own boy, anyway, Imberholt. You want to keep an eye on him. Locks and padlocks fascinate him. Not a good sign.'

Adam turned to look at her in surprise. 'How can you think it was Imberholt's child?' he asked. 'Was it likely?' he asked the man, and noticed embarrassment in his face. Coraleen must have known how it would be. How could she be so clumsy, flinging that question at her uncle's servant?

'Well, never mind,' he said impatiently. 'I'll get her out.'

'I'd better come with you, to make sure you don't run into any more trouble,' she drawled. 'Better still, I'll follow you in my car, or take you home in it. I'm sure Vic would like to test everything to see his son hasn't made off with anything.'

'A joke's a joke, Coraleen,' Adam said. 'Drop it, please,' and got his car out. He left her standing beside Vic Imberholt. He hoped she wouldn't keep on about it. He strove to remember what was wrong with the

Imberholt boy, but he hadn't had any reason to think anything about it before this moment.

Anyway, he didn't want to think about that or about Coraleen, but about Beth Kennington.

So that little nurse was going to marry the solicitor. He found he didn't care much for the idea, and told himself that the most unlikely couples mixed and matched well in time. It wasn't any of his business, anyway, and he'd have to be less fierce with her, he supposed, in case she told Quested and he made a fuss. It would be very awkward to have to tell him that his fiancée was not going to make a very good driver.

Wasn't she? How did he himself know that, Adam reasoned. It had been a challenge, one that he had gone into with zest, and had probably been more brusque than he need have been, because she had that tendency to appear to be concentrating, but was obviously trying to settle personal problems while she was driving.

But it wasn't true. He knew it and he hoped nobody else had noticed. Something about Beth Kennington got under his skin and it was not a good sign. For better or worse, he had undertaken to act as a driving instructor and that was not the way. People would be thinking there was something rather odd about his manner to this one pupil if he wasn't careful. She might be telling all her nurse friends what a beast he was to her, and that wouldn't do. But why was he like it? He didn't shout at his other pupils or use sarcasm or frustration to get the required results.

Coraleen, too, was thinking of his manner when Beth Kennington had been mentioned. She soon left Vic Imberholt and walked round the darkening grounds thinking about the curious phenomenon of Adam looking as if he really cared about something, for once. His usual bland, well-bred manner had sadly been absent tonight. At first she had been intrigued, then puzzled. Something, or someone, had got under his skin, in a way she herself could never manage. She had the urge to see this nurse at close quarters. Not speak to her but observe her from a distance. See how she reacted to other young men around her. See how other people felt about her. Perhaps if Adam saw her in nurse's uniform, doing the drudgery that she had heard nurses in their first year were expected to do, he might not produce all fire and flame at the thought of her!

But first she must see the girl herself. Call at the Nurses' Home? No, nor wait outside in her car for a sight of the girl. Much too obvious and time consuming. But Jonathan Seagrave might help.

Her eyes narrowed as she thought of Jonathan. He was one of the consultants at the hospital, and had been interested in Coraleen some time ago. His idea of being interested was to urge her to fill her empty sophisticated existence by doing voluntary work, like pushing a trolley with magazines and writing pads to sell to the patients. She paused at the edge of the ornamental lake and shivered a little. Why hadn't she let Jonathan Seagrave pursue his courtship? It might have been amusing. And then she remembered that he had been a good ten years her senior and very good at handling tricky young women. After all, he must have had plenty of experience with the nurses, to whom he used to lecture. No, Coraleen instinctively shrank from letting him think she was still interested.

But he was the only person who could let her see that girl, without beginning to wonder what her interest was. She shrugged and went back into the house to telephone Jonathan.

He was tired, after a long day in theatre but quite amused to think Coraleen had come back of her own accord. He was even more amused when she told him that she seriously considered taking up his old suggestion of pushing the trolley. 'Voluntary work? *You*, Coraleen? Well, you snapped my head off for suggesting it once before, or don't you remember? Too many men-friends under the bridge since then, eh?'

'You sound smug, Jonathan. Have you got

yourself married or something since we last met?'

'Temper, temper,' he reproved. 'And no I haven't got myself "married or something", whatever that might mean. How come you want to do voluntary work now? You didn't when I once suggested it.'

'You rushed me,' she pouted. 'I have to have time to think. Now I'd like to do it.'

He put his feet up on the table in his small room in Residents. He wished he had let his mother move house down south so that he could have lived at home, instead of having to make a monthly journey to see her and the rest of the family, and either live in, or have the crass bore of finding a flat in this dreary town. 'Well, you're unlucky, pet, because we have our full quota of trolley-pushing ladies, and I'm not sure you would have the patience to deal out small change to sick people. Not your line exactly. Of course, if you felt like doing some other kind of useful thing, there are some chaps who haven't got any visitors. Care to take them on?'

'Why haven't they got any visitors?' she asked suspiciously.

'They came in on a football coach from Aberdeen or somewhere too far for their families to visit regularly. No, forget it.'

'I'll take the job,' she said quickly. 'Will you show me round? Now don't say apply to Matron or the ward sister. Those starchy females terrify me!'

The idea of any woman terrifying Coraleen was intriguing but he fell in with her mood. She was up to something as usual, and it might be as well to find out what. Also, he recalled that her father had amassed quite a lot of money in various ways. Money was a thing that Farmansworth General Hospital hadn't got a lot of. They had been waiting for a very long time for the local Group to get their share of cash to finance essential repairs to various roofs. While that was hanging fire, nobody had a hope in the world of getting reading lights put in for patients and student nurses, but if someone could be persuaded to make a present of such things it would be well worth while; and the gentleman, if he were anything like his niece, might like to see his name acknowledged for his generosity. Jonathan leaned back in his chair, his rangy figure relaxed, his dark craggy face beginning to show signs of needing the attention of his electric razor again, after operating since four in the morning, but he thought only of how to put it to Coraleen, still chattering on the other end of the line.

'How would you like me to take you on a guided tour through the whole of the Men's Wing?' he asked lazily. 'I daresay I can fit it in.'

'I don't want to see horrific sights,' Coraleen said quickly.

'What *do* you want to see?' he asked softly.

'I'm not quite sure,' she said in her little girl voice she kept for people like Jonathan who was inclined to over-ride her sometimes. 'I do know a student nurse called Beth Kennington, and I thought it would be one up to me if she caught sight of me being useful for once. I wouldn't want to speak to her, because it would look as if I'd laid it on. But if she were to casually see me doing something or other—?'

Jonathan snorted with delighted laughter. 'This I must see, angel, and I shall extract as payment, you for a dinner date that evening. Never mind what the current escort thinks about that.'

What on earth was Beth Kennington like, Jonathan wondered, two days later, when Coraleen turned up in a mink coat against the biting cold of a late Spring day. Mink, he reflected, was an odd thing. It came in the formal dowager type of coat his mother wore and it could be styled as a modern coat with a half belt at the back as Coraleen was sporting, over velvet bell-bottoms, and a hat like the peaked cap still favoured by his mother's odd job man, but trimmed with more mink.

Mink was the Mecca of the young nurses, too, but the male patients seemed more interested in the perfume Coraleen used, and the aura of the glossy magazine which seemed to perpetually cling to her. Her hair was styled like a boy's with a gimmicky curl arrangement that appeared to be glued to each cheek. Jonathan hated it, and while he talked easily to Coraleen, and the men, his eyes roved among the young nurses who were trying to rush all their jobs to a finish and scramble for the safety of the sluice or linen room before they were caught on the wards with a consultant present with a plushy visitor in tow. The last girl to try and beat a hasty retreat, dropped the heavily laden tray she was carrying. Glasses, bottles, kidney bowls, carafes, everything on that tray scattered, with a mingling of sounds of breaking glass and china, the peculiar sharp noise with which metal met the floor or juddered against the metal legs of the beds, and the slopping of spilled water. All eyes, it seemed, were turned to the girl, whose face was scarlet to the ears, but who caught the eye of the most bandaged and splintered man in the room and grinned comically at him because he looked so anxious for her sake.

That grin caught at Jonathan's imagination. He had never seen anything quite so puckish nor rueful nor utterly good-humoured and he didn't really need the comments of the men to tell him that this was the girl that Coraleen wanted to see or be seen by.

'Nurse Kennington's in the soup again!' the men told each other, and two swung out of bed to find their sticks and crutches, with a view to helping her. Two other young nurses shot out of the kitchen and began to scramble things together. 'Beth, why don't you forget those driving lessons of yours for once?' one scolded. Staff stormed on to the ward, but the young nurse didn't show any temper at the dressing down she got in front of everyone. She went on gathering the mess together at top speed, pausing only to say, 'Yes, Staff, sorry, Staff!' and then to look pointedly across to where Jonathan and his visitor stood.

Coraleen was openly grinning, Jonathan saw. The men didn't like it and neither did he, he found himself thinking. He did a quite unprecedented thing. He left Coraleen and strolled over to the mess. 'All right, Staff,' he murmured, 'I'll carry this heavy tray for Nurse,' and before everyone he bent and took the tray of smashed bits from Beth, and they both rose together. Beth's face was more scarlet than before, but she caught sight of both their hands gripping the tray at either side, and her mouth struggled not to laugh. Jonathan appreciating the funny side of it too, murmured, 'Shall we toss for it? Oh, here comes Sister. Scoot!'

The Staff Nurse settled things by indignantly taking it from the pair of them, and left the floor undisputed to another student nurse who was trying to mop up the mess, and who would no doubt get the brunt of Sister's tongue.

Jonathan went back to Coraleen. 'That was the girl you wanted to see,' he said easily. 'Satisfied? Then let's go. I think we have worn out our welcome on this ward.'

Coraleen was only too ready to agree. Most of the men were elderly, and none of them really interested in her, since that idiot girl had dropped the tray and apparently thought it very funny. She let Jonathan take her off the ward, but wasn't prepared for him to buttonhole one of the senior nurses, whose glasses and buck teeth didn't endear her to Coraleen. 'This is Miss Drew,' he said easily. 'Nurse Wren, who has been with us many years,' he told Coraleen. 'You will have a lot in common, Nurse, when I tell you Miss Drew is terribly eager to see your charges, and to do anything to help.'

Nurse Wren grinned widely, which didn't improve her claim to good looks. 'Oh, good show, sir. I can do with some help. We'll find you an overall, dear, come on. What fun!' and she took Coraleen's arm and went charging along the corridor and up many stairs. By the time she was at the top and winded, the furious Coraleen had come to the conclusion that Jonathan had played a handsome trick on her, and turned her over to one of the older, zeal-filled nurses in the Gereatric Wing, who wouldn't let her get away with just sitting talking to one patient, she was sure. Just wait till I get him to myself again, she seethed.

Jonathan went back to speak to the Staff Nurse, fondly believing he wouldn't hear any more from Coraleen. 'I say, about that nurse and the crash, it wasn't her fault. It was mine. Very inconsiderate of me to barge in like that before they'd finished, with a visitor, only the lady's father will probably be donating something the nurses are needing pretty badly, soon.'

This sort of thing endeared him to the nursing staff. 'Oh, it's all right, sir,' Staff Nurse said. 'You can't get that girl down. She loves her life in hospital. I only wish someone would teach her to drive a car so she would have no worries outside.'

'Perhaps someone will grant you your wish, Staff Nurse,' he smiled, as he strolled off.

Beth had other problems just then, such as Howard's weekly letter, and being moved from the Women's Ward. She was kept late for her time off by the ward sister, too, who wasn't so prone to be overcome by the fascinating Mr. Seagrave, and decided to give Beth a lecture as well, on the folly of loading a tray with breakable things when she wasn't sure she could rely on her friends having remembered to straighten the casters of the bed legs. By the time Beth had got off duty, her intention of acceding to Rose Carver's wish that Beth visit her aunt, was likely to be blocked. Beth had no transport. Rose, of course, didn't think of such a thing. She herself drove an ancient car when it was willing to go, and when it wasn't, Rose was quite happy to walk across fields and take short cuts through woods. She had forgotten that young nurses had to rely on a very tricky bus service.

Beth couldn't disappoint Rose; she was such a nice person. So she looked for someone to give her a lift, but even the boiler-man's nephew appeared to have gone.

'Better watch out there, nurse,' the porter warned her. 'You might argue that Jim's van doesn't come into the New Rule but believe me, it does,' which didn't help, as Howard had already given the same warning in his last letter to Beth. 'I'd take a bus!'

'Which bus?' Beth fumed. 'I want to go to Pockling Parva.'

She stomped towards the bus stop with the intention of picking up anything that came, working her way towards Rose Carver's home village, and perhaps some kind person would offer her a lift from then on. Beth's was the unworrying nature that concentrated on getting to a place and rarely taking into consideration that the return journey was as yet unprepared.

She thought about how it would be if she had a car and was driving it herself, without

L-plates. The thought of Adam Harcourt at the wheel was inevitable, and surprising since her usually calm interior began to feel decidedly off at the mere thought of him taking her for a drive. She thrust him out of her thoughts and pondered instead on what would be the best thing to do for Staddlecombe if and when she passed her Driving Test in the stipulated time. The other things she had in her favour sealed up the inheritance: things like being a nurse which took care of the medical side, and things like being the 'steady' of a solicitor, who would of course, be able to do things like successfully running the Estate. It was just a matter of learning to drive, which meant practising driving every day, only she hadn't a car of her own and nobody to lend her one. Certainly it would be no use asking Howard to let her practise on his sleek beloved chariot, she thought with a reminiscent grin.

Jonathan Seagrave saw the grin first, and recognised the girl a second later, and changed down to run along the side of the pavement gently tooting on the horn. 'Want a lift to wherever you're going, Nurse?' he asked matily.

She flushed, thinking he was getting at her, because of that scene on the ward. The consultants did not offer lifts to the young student nurses. Then he stopped grinning, became impatient which she understood, and snapped, 'Well, make up your mind, nurse, or I'll have that Traffic Warden getting too interested in my movements,' so she said, 'Yes, please, sir, Pockling Parva if you're going that way!'

'I'm not, but it suits me fine. Hop in,' he said, his good humour restored. Beth hopped in, caught her foot in the door, and fell in an unglamorous heap against him. One strong arm guided her back into the seat by the driver, he leaned across and shut her door, and disregarding her again scarlet face, drove out of Farmansworth High Street before she plunged him into any other delicate situation. Already a bunch of First Year nurses were regarding them with high interest and it would be all over the hospital in no time.

'Never mind apologising,' he told her cheerfully, as they left the town behind. 'Tell me why you're going to the most inaccessible village I know.'

'To see the aunt of one of my patients,' Beth said in surprise.

'Have you no other transport? I mean, how were you intending to get there before I came along?'

'Bus, I suppose,' she said glumly. And then she caught sight of the way he glanced at her, his eyebrows raised quizzically, and she saw the funny side of it and chuckled. She had a low fat chuckle—infinitely contagious—and he laughed too. 'Do you always let the return

41

journey take care of itself, Nurse?'

Sobering, she said, 'Well, perhaps, but with good reason. I mean, I know lots of people, and they know lots of people and . . . well, there always seems to be someone who knows someone who will get me back to the hospital. People are very good to nurses, you know,' she finished seriously.

Well, yes, they would be good to Beth, he was prepared to concede, and thought of his grandmother and what she was very fond of saying: that the world was full of two kinds of women, the taking kind and the giving kind. That was how she would describe Beth Kennington, he saw, his thoughts clarifying. That was it: the giving kind. It exuded from her. That was how she got through life, without much preparation. She didn't have to. She gave of what she had, and things came back to her, a thousandfold. The journey was spent in silence, while he worked out how he could see her again in a natural way.

'Scoot and get your visit over, Nurse,' he said, as they went slowly down the leafy, overgrown lane that led into the back of the village of Pockling Parva, which had been neatly pushed off the map by the main road by-passing it. Pockling Parva was quiet, serene, in places picture-postcardish, and Rose Carver lived with her aunt in a thatched cottage in the centre, near the church, as became the one-time District Nurse and the

42

present teacher of the primary school. 'I'll give you half an hour, then I shall be outside blasting on the horn so don't keep me waiting and mind you tell Rose's aunt who it is.'

'But sir—'

'Oh, for heavens' sake, not while we're off duty. "Mr. Seagrave" will do, if you can't manage "Jonathan",' and he laughed as her outraged face turned round to him. 'And don't fail to come back to this car because I've a thing or two I want to say to you. Off you go!'

She got out and ran the last few yards, to the gate, and tripped on one of the loose bricks in the front path. Her face scorching, she reached the front door and fell in because Rose's aunt had seen her coming and gone to open the door in welcome. Beth took a flying leap into the hall and landed on the dog who thought it was a fine new game and roughed her until she was breathless.

'Ben! Oh, bother that dog! Get off, you silly great thing and let the poor girl get up!' Rose Carver's aunt scolded. 'I am so glad to see you, my dear. Let me dust you down. Oh, that dog gets more silly every day. Look at him! Now come into my sitting-room. Rose wrote that you might be coming so I made some fresh walnut cake that you like and we'll have a nice cup of tea. How long have you got?'

'Half an hour, to the dot,' Beth said,

pulling a face. 'One of our consultants insisted on giving me a lift. I never felt so ashamed in my life. He helped me out of a scrape on the wards when I dropped a tray and smashed things, and then today I slipped and fell on him in the car, and now this—'

'Would it be Mr. Seagrave?' Miss Frisby asked, smiling. 'I thought I recognised his car. So he's giving you a lift, is he? Oh, this rheumatism. A fine district nurse I am, if I get the complaint most of my patients suffer from!' and she slumped down in a chair, still frowning a little. 'Jonathan Seagrave. A confirmed bachelor, if ever there was one, I would have said. But still, you're a taking little thing . . .'

'Oh, Miss Frisby, it's only a lift because he wants to tell me a few things, so he said. I wouldn't be surprised if he didn't want to talk to me about that visitor of his today. I've seen her somewhere. Terribly smart. That fur coat must have cost a fortune. It's nagging at me. I wish I could think where I'd seen her.'

'Never mind, I'll pour the tea and you cut the cake, dear,' Miss Frisby said. 'And tell me about Rose, and then you can tell me about your driving lessons. Maybe I can help. I still drive a little when my limbs aren't too stiff. Better to drive than try to walk, sometimes. Why, whatever's the matter, child?'

'It's what you said,' Beth frowned. 'About

44

my driving lessons. I think that's where I've seen that awful girl called Coraleen. What did Mr. Seagrave say her surname was? Oh, yes, I know—Coraleen Drew. I think she was getting out of a gorgeous new car near the driving school one day.'

'Coraleen Drew! Well, she would be, wouldn't she, dear?' Miss Frisby said placidly, biting into her cake and shutting her mind to the thought that her rheumatism wouldn't trouble her so much if she kept to a more strict diet. 'She's Oliver Mason's niece, surely, and didn't I read somewhere that Oliver Mason is buying up other small driving schools, to amalgamate them all under one heading?' Miss Frisby chuckled. 'Are there any good-looking young men likely to be taking lessons, because that girl never bothers to visit her uncle unless there is a good-looking young man around somewhere.'

Beth mumbled something and went on eating her cake, though it now tasted like sawdust. There was only one really good-looking young man likely to interest that Coraleen Drew, she thought miserably, though why on earth she should care one way or the other about the odious Adam Harcourt, she couldn't imagine.

CHAPTER THREE

Rose's aunt sent things back to Rose in Beth's willing arms, and extracted a lot of news and information from Beth before she let her go. She also gave Beth some special ointment her friend the local chemist had made up for her. 'Rub it into your feet after a warm bath, dear. I can still remember how I felt as a very young nurse at the end of a long, long day. All I could think of was that my feet were killing me. Of course,' she chuckled slyly, 'there wasn't a consultant who gave me lifts, but then I didn't look like you do, dear.'

'How do I look?' Beth asked, rather belligerantly.

'I can't say, exactly.' Miss Frisby wasn't very good at words. 'Different from most girls, of course. Rather taking, I suppose. I only know that if I were a young man, I wouldn't let you run around loose. Oh, but I remember! Rose did tell me you were going out with a solicitor, or am I thinking of somebody else?'

Beth admitted to the truth of that, and told her enough about Howard to make her see that that young man would lose his position as first in Beth's life if he couldn't manage to seem more interesting, soon. 'He sounds a worthy young man,' Miss Frisby said.

'Oh, yes, he is. My mother says he'll make a good husband.'

'Oh, yes, I see,' Miss Frisby agreed, and went to find some buns she had made and stowed away in a plastic box ready for Beth to take back with her. 'I was always hungry in my first year,' she smiled.

So Beth hurried out at the first sound of Jonathan's horn, and clutched her parcels with determination. She didn't want to fall down again. She wasn't sure she liked Jonathan's sense of humour, and anyway, you never could trust a consultant when you were only in your first year.

He waved briefly at Miss Frisby as he passed her cottage, then he turned his attention to Beth. 'Now then, I've been thinking. Patients usually tend to believe a consultant is deaf, dumb and blind when he comes on the ward. I don't know why. But the minute you mentioned your driving lessons, I recalled hearing a lot of heated discussion going on about them. Aren't you much good?'

'Sometimes,' she admitted guardedly. 'Sometimes not good at all. It depends.'

'On what?'

'On who I get to teach me. I did very well with dear old Mr. Brown and now there's this horrible Adam Harcourt who puts my back up and positively *wills* me to do bad things.'

'Rubbish!' But he couldn't help laughing.

47

He'd like to be invisible and see what went on in that car. Sparks would fly, he thought, with a side glance at Beth. 'A person can either drive or she can't. And don't think I'm working up to let you have a try at this car because I'm not!'

'Oh, no sir, I wouldn't want to . . . I wouldn't dare!' The alarm was so patent that he began to hugely enjoy himself.

'But there is a smallish and rather older car at home. I might be prevailed on to take you out and see if you'll ever be a driver. If not, then I'll tell you so and you can pack it in, because I am persuaded that you are good nursing material and we can't get enough of those, but there are already too many drivers on the road.'

'Oh, sir, I can't just pack it in! It goes deeper than that! It isn't just a matter of driving, though of course I'd want to when I pass my Finals and go on the District . . .'

'Ride a bike,' he said, with decision. 'Anyone can do that!'

'No, sir,' she insisted. 'It's not just getting about. It's . . . oh, I didn't want to tell anybody, but the fact is, it's Staddlecombe. If I can pass my Driving Test first shot, I stand to inherit that house.'

He glanced sharply at her, and looked for a place to pull in off the road. 'This is far too serious to discuss, while driving. I want to give it my full attention,' he told her, and parked the big car in the entrance to a farm gate. Trees interlaced overhead and when the engine was shut off, the silence hit the ear-drums. Only the birds, and the sound of water trickling over stones. Beth eased out visibly and looked round her in appreciation. 'Lovely. A bit like Staddlecombe,' she murmured.

'Yes, well, do what most young people don't and begin at the beginning,' Jonathan Seagrave commanded, sitting back and stretching his long legs.

'It's very simple,' Beth said, almost undoing him again, with the comical earnestness in her face and the mere suggestion that anything with which she was connected could possibly be very simple. He kept his face straight with difficulty because she was looking at him. 'Old Mr. Unwin was a patient in our hospital for a while before he was discharged. Because it was a car accident, he said he wouldn't leave the place to some young person without they passed the Driving Test first go, because they were liable to do lunatic things. It isn't really fair, I suppose, because I believe at least one of the three other contenders has been driving for some years, only I believe Mr. Unwin considered a driver of experience to be quite safe.'

Jonathan nodded encouragingly. 'So you think you might inherit just by passing your

Driving Test?'

'Oh, no.' She was shocked at the mere thought. 'There were at least two other conditions. Being an invalid for so long he set a big store on a connection with medicine, and I passed that, being a nurse. And then there was this thing about the person inheriting knowing something of how to manage the Estate, and the solicitor said I was all right for that, too, on account of being engaged to marry a solicitor.'

'I see. But you would lose your position there, if you broke your engagement, I suppose?'

'Well, it isn't likely, sir,' she said quickly. 'About as unlikely as to say I'd soon get engaged to someone else who qualified in that field, because I'm personally no good at figures and things.'

Again he had to struggle to keep a straight face, because her earnestness over such a point was very funny indeed. He wondered what there was about her. He had seen just such blue eyes and not been very much impressed with their owners; but it was something in the way she looked at him that held his attention. He had seen just such a pretty face, and wasn't impressed by mere prettiness, but this child's face was like a mirror of changing expressions and heaven save him, he thought, in comic helplessness, he had never seen a face less touched by what

50

his grandmother pleased to call boldness, a much better word, he considered, than the modern terms that embraced the average trendy young woman, who started off a friendship with the other sex with certain thoughts and invitations bursting to the surface within minutes of the introduction. No, Beth was . . . he baulked at the word, especially in a young nurse who must have surely seen everything and heard everything, but there it was . . . she was innocent. He was quite prepared to believe that she hadn't given a thought to what might lie on the other side of taking the marriage vows, and as to her courtship . . .

'Do I know this young solicitor to whom you're engaged?'

'I shouldn't think so, sir. It's a small firm in Farmansworth belonging to his family. He is Howard Quested.'

'That chap!' He thought of that rather wintry young man. Yes, he wouldn't do anything but the correct thing with his girl-friend, Jonathan was sure. Hastily he added, 'My family did have some business with your chap's grandfather once. Yes, old Seth was . . . a bit different from young Howard, I believe.'

Beth bridled. Somehow Jonathan, by his tone, had made Howard seem an inexperienced boy. Well, he was, she supposed, but she amended that. He was what she wanted. His prosaic weekly letter was just right, though she might not have been so happy if she had known that Howard had deliberately omitted to mention dining with Oliver Mason and the reference that had been made to herself.

Being engaged to Howard presented no problems of any kind. She thought fleetingly of the uncomfortable sensations she had experienced in her very brief time of knowing Adam Harcourt and decided she was a lucky girl to have such a cool, untroubling sort of person as Howard in her own private life. Nothing to worry about in any way, until she absolutely had need to, and that thought brought the rich warm colour to her pale cheeks in a way that made Jonathan wonder.

Just what had young Beth been thinking of, he asked himself, to make her blush like that? He decided to give himself the pleasure, at some other time, of course, of finding out.

★　　　★　　　★

Jonathan Seagrave hadn't been aware that in all that conversation, Beth hadn't mentioned the fourth condition. In some ways she was inclined to be casual, brush certain things aside if she didn't believe they concerned her, and this, she thought, was well beyond the boundaries of things that need worry her. It was the question of scandal. The old man,

Maurice Unwin, had had an extremely unhappy life, through the touch of scandal, and in his last hours he was determined that nothing must stain the name of the heir, which might be deemed to be scandal, and in his narrow way he made the condition to exclude any mention in the press of the person who finally inherited his fortune and Staddlecombe. The mere thought of any derogatory mention of a person's name in a newspaper had always inflamed him.

That last conversation with his solicitor before the Will had been drawn up and signed, had not gone smoothly. His solicitor, a realist, had thought it was too tall an order, and he foresaw that he would have to draw a very careful line between what might be construed to be scandal or not. He knew that there had been scandal of a kind, in the life of at least one of the contenders but it was no use trying to tell the old man. He wouldn't listen: his time was short and he wanted to do all the talking.

In his heart, the solicitor thought that the old man had already made up his mind which one of the four would be his heir. It rested with one of two of the four contenders, and the solicitor agreed with him, that is if his guess about the old man was right. And now, unknown to Beth, the solicitor was watching everybody with a rather eager eye.

Beth went back to her work on the wards,

and didn't think very much about the consultant. It was a tiresome episode and all she wanted to do now was to keep out of his way and to keep out of the way of Coraleen.

Coraleen Drew did rather bother Beth, she had to admit. She decided that the next time she went for a driving lesson, she was going to find out just what the connection with Coraleen Drew was. Was it possible that she was the niece of Oliver Mason? But of course, as just one of the newer pupils of the school, Beth had only seen Oliver Mason in the distance. She usually made up her mind on the first glance, whether she liked a person or not, and she had certainly made up her mind quickly on seeing him. She didn't like him at all. She considered him a rather slippery character, and dismissed him. But that girl Coraleen Drew had been hostile. Beth knew she must find out why, but from whom? Not Adam Harcourt—he was so bad-tempered—

But the next time she went for a driving lesson, Adam Harcourt seemed to be rather pleasant. It completely threw her. She couldn't know that Adam had been thinking over that unfortunate dinner that he had attended at Oliver's house, and that he was unhappy about the merging of the two driving schools—the Ace and the one that Oliver was intending to buy—and in his heart, too, he was rather annoyed with himself for having let himself be talked into being a driving instructor. His old job had been pressurised, left him no private life and it had been dull but he had been at least on his own. He didn't have to get involved with people's personalities so much, and he didn't like Coraleen's trick of breathing down his neck all the time. There she was, waiting for him, at the end of each day, when he came off work, and he had to admit that although he was an experienced driver he found the days at the Ace Driving School extremely nerve-stretching and mentally exhausting. He hadn't really thought that there were people who could do the dreadful things to the controls that they did in the Ace cars. He loved cars and he didn't like to have to sit there while the gears were slammed and torn and the engine roared and stalled; and the way they stamped on the pedals needed to be seen to be believed. Whether from blind panic or bad manners, most of the pupils did their best to shorten the lives of the very good cars belonging to the school. They were a lot of vandals, he told himself angrily. No, that wasn't right, they were just amateurs. People he was employed to turn into good drivers. *Good* drivers?

He asked himself, this particular day when he was waiting for Beth, how you could tell if a person was going to be a good driver or not, and he had to admit that it *was* possible to tell. It might seem unfair but there could only be a very few people who would keep hammering away at it because they wanted to do the thing properly and turn out to be an average good driver. No, what he was meaning was, how could you recognise the born driver, the one who would be so smooth and unhurried and correct with his movements; who anticipated ahead; in short, the man who made an art of driving, and who always drove by the book all his life because he loved driving for driving's sake. There were very few of them but you could recognise them a long way off and he regretted that he'd started thinking on these lines because he had to admit in his heart that Beth Kennington was not one of them.

She would be dogged, she might even pass her Test first time if she wanted to badly enough, but *did* she? He decided to talk to her about it this day and so he greeted her with a half smile and told her it was a fine day.

Beth knew all about people who started off telling her what the weather was like. She was at once suspicious.

She said, 'I'd rather have less sunshine. I don't like the glare in my eyes.' That was unanswerable so he abandoned the subject, and settled her in the driving seat, and merely winced silently when she bumped off the clutch in starting. He let her drive on a bit without commenting. No, she just wasn't going to make a good driver.

He said quietly, 'Bring your foot slowly up off the clutch each time and remember it's the last half inch that counts.'

Beth had never heard that before, and she took her eyes off the road to look at him in some surprise.

'Watch the road!' he shouted, and that made her settle down. He was no longer polite and suave, but shouting and normal again.

I will do well now, she promised herself. But her reverse was outrageous this morning. How could anybody who had learned how to do a proper reverse round a corner that wasn't too sharp, into a side road that wasn't too narrow, make such a botch of it, he asked himself. What was worse, she would never believe him when he told her how badly she was positioned at the finish, so this morning he said, 'Put your handbrake on, and the gear in neutral, and get out and look at how the car is positioned yourself.'

He got out too, and they solemnly looked at the position. A car crept up behind them, wanting to pass and turn into the main road, but of course there wasn't room. Her face flamed with mortification, and she returned to the car, refrained from slamming the gears, and quietly turned round the corner into the main road and parked neatly, with frigid precision, and sat there fuming, waiting for

Adam to comment on her performance.

Not a propitious moment in which to stage his 'little talk', but it would have to be now, he supposed. He sat thinking about how he would begin, and met her enquiring blue eyes stormily regarding him, so he said quietly, 'You didn't ever tell me why you were so anxious to pass this Test. I didn't actually believe that it was only because of going on the District.'

'It isn't your business!' she said fiercely. 'It's just your business to get me through this Test and I'm willing to put in extra work on it if I could afford the lessons but I can't and there isn't anyone who will let me practise on his car or go with me and . . . !'

'Tell me what's the rush and I'll see if *I* can help you,' Adam said, slowly and carefully, and he stopped staring in frustration at the roof of the car and brought his eyes round to hers. His look was level and serious and had none of the anger in it that she had seen before but it was such a direct look and it made a storm of excitement rush up in her and retreat again so that she couldn't think of anything else but to ask herself why her adrenalin should work overtime or her heart smarten up its pacing and all the other medical facts which she knew were wrong. And she blamed Adam Harcourt for deliberately needling her, as usual. But then, of course, there was the point that if he was

58

going to arrange somehow to practise driving, it was what she wanted, wasn't it, so she said to him furiously, 'I have to pass my Driving Test the first go in order to inherit a house. Staddlecombe,' she said for good measure.

The way he received that information completely took her by surprise. He whitened, his eyebrows shot up and he looked so astonished that she wondered what on earth was the matter with him. 'Well, why shouldn't I be a beneficiary under a Will?' she demanded. 'The old man was a patient in our hospital. He knew me very well. I used to make him laugh.'

I bet you did, Adam thought, in appreciation. 'So you're one of the four beneficiaries,' he said.

'How did you know there were four?'

He shrugged. 'Well, you've told *me* about it. I don't suppose you've neglected to tell other people. I've heard it around. It's no secret, is it?'

'Well, it's supposed to be,' she snapped. 'We were each informed singly of the conditions. Anyway, I suppose you know who the other three beneficiaries are.'

He said, with truth, 'No, I don't,' and added, 'I don't think I want to if they're going to be as bad as pupils as you are!'

That didn't please her, either. She said, 'I only told you because you dangled the possibility of providing practising for me, in front of my eyes, and I don't believe you mean to anyway.'

'Oh, yes, I do. I keep my promises.' He gave it some thought. 'How long have you got? What's the time limit?'

'I don't know. I forgot to ask. But the solicitor knows when my Driving Test is.'

Adam said patiently, 'Do I know?' so she gave him the date. A bare month from then.

'Oh, heavens,' he murmured, half to himself. 'One month. Four weeks. Twenty-eight little days leaving out Sundays.'

'Not twenty-eight days,' she broke in sharply. 'I can't come out every day; my times won't coincide.'

'Do they give you time off to eat?'

She was sure he was getting at her now. 'Of course they do!'

'Right. Then you give up your lunch time sometimes as I do. That's if you want it badly enough.'

She was uncertain now. 'What are you going to charge me?'

He brought that gaze round to her again. She waited, bracing herself, and there it was: the rush of excitement that left her as giddy as the time when some joker at one of the hospital dances had laced her fruit punch with a double whisky. Her feet felt as if they weren't touching the ground, and every part of her tingled. She didn't know whether it was pleasurable or not. She didn't want it

60

because she just didn't understand it. And she blamed Adam irrationally for it.

'No charge. I told you so. I just want to help you.'

'Why should you want to help me?' she insisted.

'Perhaps because you're a challenge,' he said, but he said it between his teeth. That was better. She understood that, and she plunged into the fray with enthusiasm.

'What sort of a challenge? You're being nasty, aren't you?'

'Possibly,' he agreed, 'but if I don't do this, you will not get through your Test, not the first or the second or the third or fourth, or many times, and I couldn't have it on my conscience that I was such a bad teacher, I couldn't get somebody through earlier than that. So . . . fall in with my idea *if you please*. I am not charging. I am doing it as labour of . . .' He baulked at the word 'love' and then said it, and there could be no misunderstanding about his meaning because he said that through his teeth too, and that she appreciated. How many times in the past had she had to do an unpleasant job and told herself gleefully that it was a labour of love when it was simply quite the reverse.

'O.K.!' she said. 'You're on! When do we start?'

'Give me your times,' he said shrugging. 'I'll manage it, somehow.'

61

'Well, I'm off after dark. That won't do, will it?' she asked doubtfully.

'Oh, why not,' he said roundly. 'You can't possibly drive worse after dark than you do in the daytime. But we'll start tomorrow with giving up lunch. It will be good for you. Perhaps you'll drive better on an empty stomach.'

I'll show him, she told herself, and gave him her times off for the next seven days, which were scattered all over the place. He looked at the list with dismay but somehow, *somehow*, he would get to her if only for half an hour's practice.

He passed it back to her after noting down the times in his little book, then murmured wearily, 'Would it be asking too much of you to drive on, or would you rather I drove us back to the School?'

Out came her chin, in rage and indignation. He hadn't seen her do that before, and now he watched it in helpless fascination. She drove away from where they had been parked, and did the rest of her lesson with such a smoothness that he felt he could cheerfully have shaken her. When she pulled up outside the driving school at last, she couldn't resist a little glance at him with sheer dancing fun in her eyes and triumph. It had to be triumph. It was the best bit of driving she had ever done.

'Is it asking too much to tell me why you

can drive like that today and at no other time?' he asked wearily.

But there he had her. It would have been partly true to say she wanted to, or that she was in such a boiling temper that she had to prove something to him or perhaps it was through a bit of luck because no problems had presented themselves, trafficwise, that she couldn't deal with in that last half hour of the lesson. She didn't know. She just shrugged and said, 'Oh, I can sometimes, and sometimes I can't.'

He restrained himself from uttering the comment that leapt to his lips. There was no point in starting another fight at this stage but in his heart he thought that was the most awful rubbish he had ever heard, and he decided that she'd been getting at him, pretending to drive badly, for some reason best known to herself, perhaps just to needle him. She had a wicked sense of humour, that was quite obvious. But oh, the dancing fun, the glorious life in her face, her voice. The way that piquant face mirrored all those emotions compared with Coraleen's bored, deadpan face, staggered him.

He said, 'All right! See you tomorrow!' adding, 'At four. And be on the steps of the hospital for me to pick you up. This is being *worked in*, as a favour to both of us, get it?'

The fun fled from her face, and her brows came down sharply. She glared at him.

'Remember . . . you want to pass your Test first go,' he said softly, and smiled at her. A smile matching her own wicked one. She stared at it, fascinated, and gathered her things together. He got out and went round to open her door but she was all ham-fisted and stumbled out of the car against him, and his arms came up and he caught hers or she would have been over.

That, too, fascinated him. Coraleen might stage a fall to get into somebody's arms but there was nothing like that about this girl. It was a sheer accident and she was furious with herself because she hadn't finished up her little triumphant scene with dignity. He watched her stomp off, and he couldn't help smiling at her departing back. She really was a pet of a girl! And then he pulled himself up sharply. 'No, she wasn't—she was an irritating, infuriating, bumbling little wretch, and there would be greater sparks between them, he knew, before they had finished this crazy business. And what Oliver Mason would say, he couldn't think!

Oh, to hell with Oliver Mason, he exploded silently. He was giving up his own time, wasn't he? And Coraleen? Well, he would just have to elude Coraleen and not let her know that this was going on. And resolutely he put out of his mind just why he was doing it.

CHAPTER FOUR

Beth was, in spite of her little burst of anger, very thrilled with Adam's offer of free driving practice. She couldn't have asked for more or better help.

But when she was leaving the hospital in her free time the next day, she found Don Jeffers, her half brother, waiting for her.

Don was the sort of person that Adam Harcourt had had in mind when he was thinking of enthusiastic, perfect drivers. Don could do things with a car that made one think it was as natural to him as walking or even breathing. He had played in and out of cars all his life and now he worked in a service station. Fleetingly Beth wondered why she hadn't asked Don to help her but she dismissed the idea at once. Don had a curious sense of humour. He would teach her to do something flashy and dangerous, or certainly something that would cause her to fail her Test. He was like that—even though he knew very well that it was most important to all of them that she should get through it.

Looking at his half insolent smile on that good-looking face of his, she wondered how her mother could have had such a son. He must be very much like his father.

She said to him, 'What do *you* want, Don?'

'Oh, charming,' he drawled. 'Come to see my little half sister and what do I get?'

'Well,' she said, 'you never let me know before you come and how do *you* know I haven't got a date?'

'You haven't,' he told her with assurance.

'Yes, I have,' she flashed back. 'And I don't want you making me late now. What do you want, anyway?'

'What do you suppose I've come for, little Beth?'

'Have you come to take me out?' she asked doubtfully.

That made him laugh. 'Well, I suppose I was at that,' he hastily amended, because as he had come to ask Beth for a loan of enough money to take out his girl-friend, that night, it wasn't good sense to refrain from being nice to Beth.

She said, 'Well, I'm sorry but I can't wait now because I've got a driving lesson, and if you know what's good for you, for heaven's sake help me to get through this Test.'

'Isn't it getting a teensey bit boring, all this talk about this Driving Test of yours, love?' he mused, turning round to walk beside her.

'Go back, Don! I don't want you with me!'

'Oh,' he said. 'Got a new bloke, have you? And what would old Howard say?' but Beth could already see Adam in the driving school car. Don followed her glance and said, 'Oh, it *is* a driving lesson! Oh, well, keep up the

66

good work, love,' and he swung away in the opposite direction and went off whistling. She breathed a sigh of relief and hastened down to where the car was waiting.

But Don just hung around until he saw her drive off, also closing his eyes and wincing, just as Adam did, at the way she thought a car had to be driven away from the kerb. She had to brake hastily to let an overtaking car pass her because she'd forgotten to look over her shoulder at the 'blind spot' and Adam had purposely waited to see if she would and left it a fraction too long. That made him furious, too, because he had been guilty of not watching out this day. He was too busy thinking over that last scene with Coraleen. He was worried, too, at the way he had felt when he saw Beth come away from that young man.

What a coil they were all in! He said irritably, 'For heaven's sake forget your boy-friend and concentrate on what you are doing,' and Beth retorted smartly, 'It's not my boy-friend, it's my brother. I didn't want him there and he always annoys me.'

Annoyed further with himself, Adam recalled that the solicitor was Beth's fiancé. 'Well, calm down,' he snapped, 'if we're going to make any sense out of this practice business. Now settle down,' so with a tremendous effort she pushed Don out of her mind. He had been leaving the hospital amenably enough. What had she got to worry about? But it had only just struck her at that moment that he had merely come to borrow money. Would he ask anyone else for some, on the grounds that he had just missed his sister? Such a thought made her so frightened that she just kept on trying to turn round the corner in third gear, and felt the dual controls tug as Adam took over. He got the car round the corner by leaning over and using the wheel himself, and then pulled in to the side.

'What . . . is . . . the . . . matter?' he asked through his teeth.

She was near tears of frustration. 'Just let me get my breath,' she gasped, 'and then I'll start again.'

'You'd better!' he said.

Don. Where was he going? Who would he speak to? Was it worth continuing this particular practice session? Hadn't she better go back and find out what he wanted? Money! Why hadn't she thought of it and given him some? What else would he want of her? And then it struck her that such a course wouldn't have been possible because it was the end of the month and she had hardly got enough to get through herself. She thrust him out of her mind with such an effort that it left her weak and shaking, and resumed the driving again, and this time she drove reasonably well.

'That's better!' Adam approved and he

68

took her to the nursery streets to practice that absurd turning round backwards in the car.

Sometimes he came near to believing that he had a flair for teaching but at other times his own irritation against the person in the driver's seat built up into a solid lump and he couldn't think of the way to persuade that person to do the thing properly. But Beth was different. It was quite clear that she wanted terribly to be good at this, so he put his hand on hers as it grasped the wheel, and said, 'Let's begin right back at the beginning. I'll show you first, the right way to hold the steering wheel.' He was sharply aware that her hand was trembling under his, and that he was shaken himself at the touch of her hand. He hastily snatched his own hand away.

'Look at the car,' he invited, 'as a piece of machinery that you are going to make *do* things. Can you give a person an injection?' he asked, on sudden inspiration.

Her face lit. 'Yes. I've just learned how, and I do it perfectly, Staff Nurse says.'

He nodded, never doubting that she was telling the truth. 'Well,' he said, 'I couldn't give a person an injection to save my life. It seems to me the most difficult thing on earth.'

'Oh, it isn't!' she told him, her face still lit in a way that he couldn't tear his eyes from it. 'Mind you, you have to know what you're doing and you must have nerve.'

69

'Just what I thought,' he said calmly. 'And that is how you approach driving a car. You do not let it take itself all over the road as you seem to think it does. You take it where you want to. And now we'll have a little practice at going back, in a civilised way. A child could do no worse than you usually do. Now let's take it sensibly.'

'Sensibly' was a word Beth understood, and she appreciated having a thing put to her as a challenge, especially when compared with something she was doing on the wards, and this time she got the reversing right. But in her heart she was convinced that the next time she came to do it, very likely she wouldn't get it right. But she was so touchingly thrilled when she brought the car in level with the kerbside, that he wanted to hug her. She was such a baby, really, and so rewarding a pupil when she was in this mood. But he was still faced with the extraordinary astonishment that anybody could find it difficult to cause a car to run backwards slowly in a straight line. To him it was the easiest thing on earth. He had done it when quite a schoolboy, messing about with the cars at home.

However, that was not Beth's problem. Beth had not long been driving, apparently, in the last few months. But that half an hour which he was able to give her that day went very easily and very well; she had had a

70

success and she wanted to keep it up, and for the moment Don was forgotten.

Don, however, was doing such things that if Beth had known, she wouldn't have even stayed in the driving school car, but would have run all the way back to the hospital.

Don had the bright idea of strolling over to the Nurses' Home, and hanging about there. In a little while Beth's two friends came out. Grace looked on him with no great favour. She had seen him before, and she knew that Beth hadn't very much patience with him. But Frances was the sort of girl who liked the look of any young man provided he was healthy and didn't wear glasses. Poor health and poor sight in a young man were her two *bête noirs*. Howard was the one kind of young man that Frances couldn't stand and she often wondered privately how it was that Beth could be content to go out with Howard when she'd got a brother who looked like this.

Grace left them with a muttered: 'See you!' and marched off, but Frances waited for him to reach her and said pleasantly, 'I'm afraid you've missed Beth. She's gone out.'

'Oh, dash,' Don said. 'She promised to lend me a fiver.'

Frances' eyebrows shot up. 'She did *wha-at?*' she exclaimed. 'It's the end of the month! Don't be silly, she hasn't got a bean. She had to borrow from me to get her lunch yesterday.'

'*Oh*. Then I've had it,' Don said ruefully. 'Oh, well, nothing for it but to take a little loan out of the till, I suppose. Oh, it's all right—the boss won't mind. But I don't like doing it. I've got principles, you see.'

Frances was shocked. 'You can't do that! You *can't* be so hard up.'

'Well, no, I'm not,' he allowed, 'but who wants to touch their savings? I'm saving up for something rather special,' and he looked at her in a way that he'd practised on the boss's wife and it had the same effect on Frances.

'Oh—here, wait a minute,' Frances said. 'I think I've got a couple of pounds you can have, but no more. Will that do?'

Don was inordinately grateful. He waited while she dashed into the Nurses' Home for it.

When Frances came back with the money, he asked casually, 'Where were you off to? I mean, your friend's gone off without you. Can I give you a lift anywhere? I use the firm's cars, you see. I work in a garage.'

Frances was very grateful for the lift. He brought the car up to where she waited for him. It was a big plushy model, one that he had no business to be borrowing, but she wasn't to know that.

She said, 'It's a super car. And you're a super driver!'

'Oh, well, you get used to it,' Don said

modestly. 'Won't your bloke mind? I forgot to ask you. You being picked up by a stranger, I mean.'

'Oh, I haven't any special man friend,' Frances said.

He glanced measuringly over at her. He had recoiled at first at the shower of freckles all over her face, but once you got used to her they became part of her charm. He thought she might be fun.

'You know, it may seem silly,' he mused, 'but although I needed that money so badly I wish now that I hadn't had to ask *you* for it.' He cut short her protests and said, 'I could make it up to you, if you got a bit of time off, in a way that doesn't need money, I mean. This car, for instance. How would you like a spin to the coast? Only a walk on the beach, I'm afraid, and a coffee, till funds come in, but it could be fun. What do you think?'

Frances tried to think of all the objections she could, but the only thing that bothered her was whether Beth would mind, and she couldn't think that Beth would, really. Beth had said nothing much about Don. She was just impatient of him in some way and Frances couldn't see why, really. So she agreed.

'I've got four hours,' she admitted, 'and I was wondering what to do with them.'

'The coast it is, then. A breath of sea air will do you good.'

So Don drove down to the coast, in what was for him a very circumspect manner, although Frances thought it was rather fast driving, but he was such a good driver; slick. Beth would have been very anxious if she could have seen this exhibition because she knew what Don was like when he was taking out a girl for the first time, and the way he tried to impress them.

But Beth had problems of her own. There was this curious feeling when she was with Adam. She mustn't let him see it, she thought, and that took her mind off the driving again, and she was very cross because she had wanted to do a perfect half an hour to repay him for taking her out.

He pulled up in the street behind the hospital because it was easier for her to park than in the road where he had picked her up.

Eagerly she asked: 'Well, how did I do?'

'Much better,' he allowed, 'but you don't concentrate all the time. You've got worries, haven't you?'

'Well, yes, how did you guess?' she blurted out.

'*How did I guess?*' he murmured. 'Well, let's say that you touched the kerb as you were going round the corner and one or two things like that and you don't usually do anything quite so outrageous—only half outrageous.'

She hesitated between looking stormily at

him and laughing, and the laughter won. 'I know,' she said. 'I'm awful. Oh, but I must try somehow. I wonder if I could get rid of all my other worries and then give all my mind to my driving, it would answer?'

He said, 'Do the things you have to do on the ward worry you when you're driving?'

That surprised her. 'Oh, no! No, I really love my work on the ward. No, that doesn't worry me at all. In fact,' she admitted, in a burst of confidence, 'I don't think that anything I could do on the ward would worry me. I know I do awful things, of course. I had a terrible smash-up with a tray of stuff the other day but that sort of thing doesn't worry me. The rule is that you clear it up as quickly as you can and stay good-humoured so that Sister doesn't become more wild than she is, and then it's all over, and if you don't get in a terrible state and get cross or anything, the patients think it's funny and the main thing is to think of the patients.'

He nodded. Yes, she would think that way. And then he thought to himself, Careful! You're thinking this way about her again and it *won't do*. So he said, 'Well, whatever worries you've got, you'd better think them over, before we meet tomorrow, and if it will help to get them off your chest, just tell me about them, because it isn't any good at all, my giving up my eating time and you giving up your time to come out and practise if your

75

attention is drawn off on something else. So let's get the worries fixed once and for all, shall we?'

She looked really bothered quite suddenly. He said sharply, 'Well, what's the matter now?'

She said simply, 'It's people. And you can't change people, you know.'

'What people?' he asked.

'My family. It would take a little time to settle their worries. Oh, but it will be all right,' she said hastily. 'I won't think about them. I promise. I don't have to. I can keep my mind clear if I want to. At least, I think I can!'

She wasn't going to give any more confidences now, and of course there wasn't time now, not for either of them. He had to hustle off and pick up a pupil at the person's home. So he nodded, and said, 'See you do, otherwise we'll both be wasting our time, and setting up a whole new lot of tension into the bargain! See you tomorrow!' and he left her.

Beth went back to her work on the ward feeling terribly hungry. There was going to be trouble if Sister found out. Beth promised herself that she would eat a bar of chocolate with her tea and an extra helping tonight, perhaps, at the evening meal. Somehow she must work out just how she could manage this way. Perhaps she could manage to eat a sandwich before she went out to meet Adam.

Why was life so difficult?

Adam was asking himself that question. He had run into Coraleen. Her car was level with his at the next traffic lights and she didn't look at all pleased. She fell in behind him and followed him—a thing he disliked very much—and when he pulled up outside the next pupil's house, in a small back street, she parked behind him and got out with great distaste.

'What . . . are you doing, Adam?' she asked him.

'Calling to pick up my next pupil. What are you doing?' he returned.

'I've been following you round since you picked up that nurse at the hospital. I don't remember it was arranged that you should pick her up there today.'

A slow brick red flush crept under his skin and he stood there, not saying anything, but looking at her with such intense anger that even Coraleen wavered a little.

'Oh, well,' she said, 'I suppose you know what you are doing, but you usually tell me—discuss all your pupils—I thought perhaps you'd forgotten or something.'

He still stood there looking at her.

'Well, why don't you say something, Adam?'

'I'm waiting to be allowed to go and pick up my pupil,' he said. 'We'll be meeting later. We can discuss this then, surely?' and

77

he nodded to her and walked away, decisively opening and shutting the gate of the little house behind him, and standing with his back turned her way while he waited for an answer to his pressing of the door bell.

She was furious. He had never done that to her before. She had expected him to say something like: 'Darling, I can explain everything. It's been the most difficult situation and I know your uncle wants to be pleased etc.' Propitiating. She liked Adam to be propitiating. But all of a sudden he was intensely masculine, and quietly seething with anger, and it filled her with excitement.

She decided to go back to the driving school and wait for him, and then thought she wouldn't. They were meeting tonight when he came off duty. He would be tired then and less prone to argue with her and it wouldn't be so exciting, but she might be able to whip up some energy in him to oppose her again.

No, she had a better idea. She would drive him home and persuade him to leave that awful driving school car with its great L-plates and name of the school, back in the school yard.

Adam finished his work that day in a mixed frame of mind. As with Beth, it hadn't helped, going without food. They both of them put out too much mental as well as physical effort on their respective jobs and he was tired, hungry and rather bad-tempered and not at all pleased to find Coraleen waiting for him. She was crowding him, he thought with surprise. And with further surprise he realised that he had to get free. Or at least arrange to refrain from seeing her for two or three days. And how on earth could you do that with a person like Coraleen.

He said bluntly: 'I am not going to leave this car here. You know your uncle doesn't like it. If anything goes wrong with it, owing to this very poor parking here, it would be up to me to put it right and I'm not taking that extra on!'

She recognised the danger signals, and said smoothly, 'I understand that, Adam. Right, well, I'll follow you home, because I want to *talk* to you.'

'Not tonight, Coraleen. Can't you see when a chap's tired and just wants a bath and a decent meal and—'

'We can go out for a meal!' she broke in.

'No,' he said.

But Coraleen had always had that failing. She could never take a firm 'no' from a man. She'd been brought up by uncles, male cousins, men there on the scene all through her life, to twist round her little finger. A 'no' was to Coraleen a come-on sign.

She just smiled at Adam and followed him, as if he had never spoken, and when he accelerated in the school car, she caught him up with ease in her more powerful car. So that at last, when he pulled up outside what he knew to be her favourite restaurant, she almost drove into the back of him. It was going to be like that.

'Adam, you *can't* go in here looking like that!' she said indignantly. 'Why don't you go home and change?'

'Coraleen, you wanted to have a meal out. We're having a meal out. I cannot wait to go home and change. I'm ravenous!'

'What did you have for lunch?'

'Do you mind if we park the cars and go in? If you do, then I shall get in my car,' he said, with such firmness that she knew he meant it, 'and go elsewhere.' So she agreed.

They went in to have their meal in frosty silence. Coraleen was dressed for the part, certainly, but oddly enough, Adam let her pay for the meal; as Coraleen had taken over the ordering, the waiter kept his eyes discreetly averted from Adam's far from fresh shirt, and his rather untidy hair. For such a normally fastidious man, he looked as if he'd been having a rather rough day, Coraleen considered, and while they waited for the food to come, she said, 'What happened to you today?'

He looked morosely at her. 'I am working for your uncle. All day and every day I look like this, I feel like this. But usually you give me a chance to go and take a bath and cool off before we meet. If you won't grant me that courtesy, then you must expect to see me like this.'

She subsided and didn't speak again for some time, which should have warned him, but he was just grateful for the silence. And when the food came, it was good, and she allowed him to eat it in peace. She had also chosen wine which she knew he liked, and that helped him too.

When the meal was drawing to an end, however, it became clear to him that she hadn't given up. She wanted to finish things now; they were going to discuss it whatever happened.

He wondered how he could keep his voice down. Why did she push so?

'I want to know what you're doing with that nurse,' she said. 'And why it wasn't in the books. I had a look especially so I know it wasn't entered.'

'Did you report it to your uncle?' he asked.

'Well, no, I didn't.'

'Why not?'

'Well, I was sure there was some rational explanation, darling, and besides, we *are* supposed to be engaged, and you have to remember that Uncle does think an awful lot of you.'

'So why are you bothering?' Adam asked evenly.

She didn't stop to pick her words carefully, which was a mistake on her part. She said, with a low intense passion in her voice: 'Because I have to make it clear from now onwards that if we're to remain engaged I want to know everything, *but everything*, about you.'

He played with his fork, making an odd little pattern on two inches of table cloth.

'Don't *do* that!' she said, so he put the fork down, and grasped his own hands, until the knuckles shone white, and he stared at them as though he had never seen them before.

'Why don't you answer me?' she asked him.

'If you really want to know,' he said, and waited while the coffee was brought. 'If you really want to know,' he resumed when they were alone again, 'I just don't know what to say. I hadn't ever dreamed that you'd keep hammering like this.'

'I'm . . . not . . . hammering,' she said, on a low intense note.

'Is it going to be like this all the time?' he asked, in a low deceptively quiet voice.

'I don't know what you mean by "like this",' she said, rather wildly. 'Adam, what's the matter with you? You're not like yourself tonight. But I tell you this. If we're going to be married, I don't want you fooling around with any little nurse from the hospital, like *that* girl. I could tell you a thing or two about her. She flirts with everybody, and makes herself thoroughly cheap.'

'What makes you think I want to know anything about her, outside of her driving potentiality?' he asked, still in that dangerously quiet voice.

It was just quiet to her. She missed the danger note in it. 'You may not be interested now, but you will be! She's the sort of girl who gets under a chap's skin. I've seen them before. And what is more, I don't like her and I don't like you being with her. And I don't want you to have her for a pupil. You've got plenty others, and I know at least four more people who would want to learn, and I've told them about what a good teacher you are. Why don't you scrap her? She'll be no good.'

He was silent for a while, then suddenly, without looking up from his hands, he said, 'You've told me what it's going to be like in the future from your point of view, Coraleen. Now I must tell you what it's going to be like if you don't do things to please me,' and because he was still resolutely looking down at his hands, he didn't see how her face changed. Sharp surprise was replaced by a sullenness that would have shocked him.

'Go on,' she gritted.

'The thing is, Coraleen, that I must be left to feel free to please myself; which pupils I take, where I spend time, what things I do. I shall be faithful, whether as a fiancé or a husband, but I will not be dictated to.' And then he did look up at her, so swiftly, that he caught the tail end of that bitter look before she swiftly composed her features. But the look of deep hurt that she hastily conjured up was just not quite quick enough. He wasn't deceived.

'How could you say that to me, Adam?'

'I can say it to you,' he said carefully, 'because I want to preserve what is left of our engagement. I don't want it spoilt by any more of this talk. So let's give it up, shall we? You're probably tired or disappointed over something and want to have a row with me. But not here, please! Because I assure you, the way I am feeling at the moment, if we quarrel any more, in this place, I shall get up and go out. And if I get up and go out, it will be the end, between you and me.'

She gaped at him. 'You can't mean it, Adam!' she gasped. 'It's that girl. She's got you away from me. She's horrible. Do you know, she even leads the men on, the patients, on the ward. Sick and injured men. Think of it. She does, truly she does! And the consultants, too. Think of that. The way she looks at men, any man, even the porters . . . she can't leave anybody alone! There was even that poor old Mr. Brown, the instructor she had before you came on the scene. He decided to leave, poor old chap. It's being in that car together . . . Honestly, there should be a third person present, to act as a chaperone.'

She couldn't stop, once started. The only way she could still her truant tongue was to slap her hands to her mouth and hold them there.

Adam looked at her. He had meant what he said, and heavens, how he wanted to be free of her, but in that moment he saw that he would do no good to Beth if he broke this engagement, for he would have to leave the driving school, and if that happened, what could he do? Beth was engaged to someone else. It wasn't as if she were free, and he could then, in a mood of disinterestedness, coach her and take her through her Test.

He sat staring at Coraleen, not really seeing her, but seeing Beth, straining to get through her Driving Test to inherit Staddlecombe, and he thought of his own sister, who surely wouldn't thank him for letting that fine old house and the fortune with it, go to a stranger, a little nurse who was engaged to a small town solicitor. And while his thoughts held him in chains, Coraleen acted quickly so that he couldn't keep his word and go. With a soft moan, she half rose to her feet, then sank in a heap on the floor.

CHAPTER FIVE

Adam sat beside Coraleen's bed the next day and regarded her seriously. She was in her best little-girl mood, as frilly and feminine as the rest of the room, her hair released from its usual smooth and sophisticated upswept style, and bunched into thick curls at each side of her head and tied with ribbons. She looked so unlike herself with all this feminine show that Adam felt curiously embarrassed. Yet he had seen it all before. Not perhaps the nightie and matching negligee—they were new and must have set her uncle back quite a bit. Adam was a man of the world enough to have some idea what women's clothes cost. This was all laid on for his benefit, as was the studied way she lay back cuddling the great bunch of hothouse blooms he had brought for her. He too, had put on an act, insofar as this was a formal visit of formal visits, like visiting a relative in hospital. It had its set pattern of rules. It was something he knew he had to do. Whether that had been a real fainting fit or just a clever bit of acting to end a scene that hadn't gone the way she had wanted it to, he would never know and he felt too weary of it all just then to question it too far.

She said, 'Oh, Adam, you came!'

He raised his eyebrows so she said quickly,

'I'm being an awful nuisance but I feel I'm going to cry. I expect it's because I'm not very well after yesterday. What happened to me?'

He said bluntly, 'You fainted. It was as well, wasn't it?' and she looked at him and he could see that she knew perfectly well what he meant.

'Do you hate me, Adam?' she asked softly.

'I don't hate anyone at this moment.'

'Well, do you still love me?' she persisted.

He shifted restlessly. 'Oh, Coraleen, let's let things go, shall we? Let's say that whatever made you faint last night, it was as well, perhaps. We were both tired and probably disappointed with something and said a lot of things we wouldn't normally have said to each other. How about if we scrub it out, forget about it?'

She caught her breath to stop herself releasing the torrent of protests that welled up to her lips, and agreed with him. 'Yes, let's forget about it. Let's go back to the beginning and start all over again, shall we?'

'I hardly think we can do that, my dear. We've come a certain way along the road towards getting engaged. The thing is, do you want to stay engaged to me or do you want to call it off?'

'No, of course I don't want to call it off—that was the whole point,' she gasped.

'Right, then we stay engaged,' and he

added with great determination, 'Let's talk about other things. You'd better put those flowers down or they'll wilt.'

'Oh, but first—have you spoken to my uncle? Did he say anything about last night?'

'Well, he was very concerned, poor man. He looks as if he's got enough on his plate already, with business matters.'

'What did he say exactly?'

'Oh, he didn't say very much. Just that the doctor pronounced that you needed a bit of a rest and he agreed that I should come up and see you. I'm not to stay long, so I won't stay long.'

She had to be content with that and they talked of general things until he went. But his kiss had been a perfunctory one: or had it been one of those kisses a man gives to a woman who strikes him as being too frail to stand up to his normal storm of passion?

She would have liked to think so, but she was a realist enough to know that somewhere along the way, she had slipped up and come near to losing Adam. She glared at the door through which he had departed so quietly. They hadn't discussed any of the things she had wanted to and each time she had tried, and endeavoured to bring the matter inevitably back to Beth Kennington, he had adroitly steered the conversation away and Coraleen knew better than to start another fight, because this time it would be the end.

And with Coraleen, if an affair ended, she had to be the one to end it, not the man concerned. And she wasn't ready to let Adam go yet.

She lay there thinking of how much she enjoyed the feeling that other girls were looking enviously at him. He was so big, so handsome, so masculine and arrogant. It was that arrogance of his that appealed to her most of all. When he did climb down off his high horse to be nice to her sometimes, she felt curiously disappointed as if he were just like all the other men being nice to her. Predictable. But Adam being arrogant . . . yes, that was what she liked to hold on to.

She had been forced to stay in bed for the day. So much for her bit of acting last night! She hated being penned in the house, but she had the telephone beside her, and she thought she would telephone around to friends. Old friends, those she had allowed to slip away. She ran through their names, experimentally, but none of them appealed. Only one name came to mind that in any way excited her: Quentin Burgess, an old flame who had been most reluctant to go when she had got tired of him. She wondered idly if she could still draw him back into her net. She knew that he was still single. Her uncle had mentioned him recently. He had wanted to do business with him. Coraleen, as sure of herself as ever, called him up in the middle of a working day.

He was busy dictating to his long-suffering elderly secretary, and recognised Coraleen's honey-sweet tones at once. He thought fleetingly that she hadn't changed. Still self-centred enough to believe that a pretty girl could wean a man from his working life the minute she telephoned him. He snarled to the girl on the switch board that he had left orders not to be disturbed, then he altered his mind and decided to speak to Coraleen after all.

'Three minutes only, poppet,' he chuckled into the telephone, frowning at his secretary to remain where she was and not to try and escape. 'I suppose you want a wedding present out of me, is that it?'

'Long time no see,' she began, 'and what makes you think that's what I want?'

'Just something your uncle said when he invited me over to dinner tonight,' he said, with a wry smile. 'Didn't he tell you I was coming?'

She hadn't seen her uncle that day. The last time she had spoken to Oliver Mason there had been sharp words between them because her uncle had suggested she was trying to interfere with the running of the driving school. She wondered if her uncle had guessed what she was doing about Beth Kennington. She slid around that by saying 'I haven't seen him today actually. When was it arranged?'

The elderly secretary was getting edgy so Quentin said, 'Never mind that, my dear. I'll see you tonight, yes?' and put the phone down.

She lay there thinking about Quentin. She had been the one to terminate that old friendship and she wondered how it would be with him coming back into her life again. She remembered him as a big heavily made man a good ten years older than she was, but terribly sophisticated. At the time he had treated her like a tiresome little kitten, showering gifts and flowers on her but not being particularly impressed by her. She hadn't liked the way he had kissed her.

What would he be like now, she wondered? In those days she had liked her friends to be youthful. Now she liked the older men. What would he think of her now, she wondered? She fancied she had matured very much.

From Quentin her thoughts roved towards Jonathan Seagrave. He hadn't got into touch with her since she had gone to the hospital that day. She had smarted at the way he had foisted her on to that elderly nurse, and then the old light of battle had lit her eyes and she had told herself to wait, and attack him again. Her weapons were not those that Beth Kennington employed: Coraleen didn't feel the need to play fair when it came to punishing a man for the way he had treated her. She decided to telephone him. He should be off duty now. But she had never appreciated the term 'on call' and was quite surprised to learn that he was operating.

Losing her patience now, she called up other young men she knew, and learned a new fact about herself. They bored her, besotted as they were with her charms. She found she only cared about the unattainable. Only enjoyed the plotting and planning to make an unwilling man her slave and then discard him. Who was an unwilling male?

She searched her mind and remembered Paul Ingram. The solicitor of the late Maurice Unwin. A clever, self-assured man of fifty odd years, distinguished with a touch of silver in his iron grey hair, and eyes that disconcertingly read a person. Paul Ingram, yes, she must try him. What did she need a solicitor for? Well, she could always make her Will, she supposed.

It wasn't very easy to persuade him to the telephone. His wasn't a small family firm like that of the Quested family. Paul Ingram was a rather exclusive sort of lawyer, boasting an efficient and suave Managing Clerk who stepped into the breach, keeping at a distance any but those clients Paul Ingram wanted to see. The wealthy ones, like the late Maurice Unwin. She knew all this perfectly well, yet she couldn't resist dialling his number, lying there in bed. She might have luck and find the Managing Clerk out, and some idiot of a switchboard operator caught on the hop and putting her straight through.

She didn't even get the Managing Clerk, who was also engaged. The litigation clerk said vaguely that he'd see, and put the telephone down. He had been carrying a pile of papers which slipped, and scattered themselves all over the desk and floor. He picked up most of them but was called into the Managing Clerk's room to answer a question. One of the draft documents still lay where it had fallen on the telephone receiver, obscuring it but not blotting out sound. Two typists came into the room to look for a file, and Coraleen heard a curious conversation.

Evidently the switchboard operator had been doubtful about putting Miss Drew straight through to Paul Ingram and had prudently (though tactlessly) asked around, what the connection was. The girls were laughing about it. 'Well, who was it, after all?' one said, and the other one murmured, as she tugged filing cabinet drawers in and out in search of some papers she wanted, 'Coraleen Drew. What a name!'

'Would that be the Old Man's latest?' the other girl asked.

'No, don't be an ass. This one's connected with the Driving School; *that* affair, remember?'

'Oh, yes, I know—Staddlecombe!'

Coraleen resisted the urge to shout

something acid into the telephone and strained her ears. The two girls were moving out of range now but moved back again, still oblivious of the fact that the telephone was off the hook. Now she could pick up the threads again and held her breath as they began to discuss in a desultory way, the matter of the four contenders to the late Maurice Unwin's Will.

'Well, nobody's surprised to find Oliver Mason's name there, because after all, he was distantly related to the poor old boy, and just mention money and that chap's in on it like a dog on a rat.'

Coraleen's cheeks scorched. How near the bone that comment was!

'The same goes for Adam Harcourt. Related to the old boy, I mean.'

Coraleen let out a soft breath of surprise, as the unseen talkers went on, unaware. 'And we all know why Quentin Burgess got in on the band wagon, don't we?' but the other girl wasn't as au fait with the controversial Will of Maurice Unwin, so there were willing explanations, and Coraleen lay in her frilly bed, writhing as these two indiscreet people discussed the fact that Quentin was a manufacturing chemist which had probably got him past the medical hurdle in this unusual Will.

'But has he passed his Driving Test?'

'Don't be silly, he's been driving for years.

He's a super driver. I know, don't I?' and
there was more laughter. One of Quentin's
little poppets, Coraleen thought furiously.
This seemed to be born out by the whispered
conversation that went on, retailing what
went on in Quentin's car at times, punctuated
by giggles. Coraleen writhed, but had to
admit that Quentin was probably like that
with anyone's typists, his own or those of his
solicitor.

Suddenly, cutting across the silence which
followed, one of them asked, 'Who was the
fourth one in old Unwin's Will?'

'You'll never guess. It's some ghastly little
student nurse at the hospital where the old
man was. She nursed him for a time, they
say. Kennington, yes, that's the name. Nurse
Kennington.'

Coraleen lay there frozen with shock. She
didn't need Paul Ingram now—she had all the
information she wanted. But how was it she
hadn't realised that? Of course that girl would
have to pass her Driving Test first time, and
if she knew Adam, he'd get her through,
somehow. It would be a challenge he
wouldn't be able to resist. But she couldn't let
that girl inherit Staddlecombe and the Unwin
fortune! Her uncle needed it!

At the other end of the line one of the girls
said, 'Oh, look, I've been searching for that
draft Conveyance all this time and there it is,
on the table, all the time.' Then there was a

sort of gasp, no doubt as the document was lifted, to reveal the unhooked receiver. 'Who's on the phone?' Coraleen heard a scared voice ask the other one.

She quietly put her phone down. They'd hear the dialling tone and forget about it if they had any sense. She had too much to think about to bother about those two girls. She wondered if her uncle knew who the others were. Well, he'd know about Quentin. That would be why he'd asked Quentin over to dinner tonight. He probably knew about Adam—he'd know very well that Adam was distantly related to the old man, or did he? He had never mentioned it. Perhaps he didn't know! It had not been a close-knit family. Now she lay back, tense and uneasy, wondering just what chance her uncle had of inheriting Staddlecombe.

She reviewed all four of them in turn, slowly, carefully. The three men would have passed on the car driving test, surely. Quentin would be well away with his connection with the chemical manufacturing business he had inherited from his father, she supposed. But her uncle? What connection with medical things had he got? Nor for that matter, Adam? And she couldn't be at all sure about the scandal angle, either. She supposed in a worldly way that neither Quentin nor her uncle would pass that, if it was to be a stringent test combining business dealings, with a good private investigator on the job. As to Adam, he might be free of scandal but he had no knowledge of running an Estate or connection with the medical field, that she knew of.

But the Kennington girl ... Now, there was danger. She, if she could be put through her Driving Test, would satisfy on all other counts, Coraleen thought angrily. And furthermore, she foresaw that if Beth Kennington could be somehow got out of the way, she herself stood to gain in this business either through her uncle's inheriting, or by either marrying Adam or Quentin, whichever was the lucky one. Beth Kennington's position was a triple danger to Coraleen herself!

Individually her uncle was not a good bet, she went on thinking. He was, of course, madly desirous of inheriting Staddlecombe but not for a reason Coraleen liked. He wanted to turn Staddlecombe into what she supposed was really a new idea in the business world. She knew he wanted to turn it into a special kind of private hotel, just for putting up potential wealthy customers for the week-end, so that they could get their round of golf and all the amenities of an extremely plushy hotel, with the overtones of an historical mansion, but also with a boardroom and suite of offices, a fleet of secretaries, all the amenities of his London office. They would arrive, and not go until the deals had been put through. It certainly would not be kept as purely a stately home run for parties and gay times as Coraleen desired it. •

She raged silently against her uncle because she knew he would get his way if he inherited. But how could he inherit, on the two facets he possessed?

Like the other two, he hadn't a complete set of the required conditions. No, it looked as if Beth Kennington would win, with that Driving Test. Why, just why had that girl been chosen in the first place? Obviously of course the angle of looking after the Estate was taken care of by that young solicitor she was engaged to. But scandal . . . What did they know about her background? It nagged Coraleen all that day, and when Quentin came to dinner that night, she couldn't wait for an opportunity to get him alone to talk to him about it.

This didn't happen until the meal, heavy as always, had been got through, and her uncle was settled alone with his port. She urged Quentin out on to the terrace, and began without her usual working up to a subject, 'I've been thinking about this beastly business of the Staddlecombe inheritance. I only heard today that you were one of the contenders.'

It wasn't like Coraleen to be so direct and blunt. He looked rather alarmed. 'How the devil did you hear that?' he asked.

'Well, let's say I heard it by accident,' she said.

'Dirty means,' he grinned. He knew Coraleen's methods only too well.

'Does my uncle know?' she asked.

'Well, he does now,' he admitted. 'Because I really came over to discuss it with him. I don't think either of us stand a chance all the way, with those stupid conditions. And I do need that place. I've had my eye on it for years.'

She decided she'd better tell him about Beth Kennington. He heard her out in silence but finally got tired of her bitter remarks.

'It's no good your carrying on,' Quentin said, moodily staring out into the dark grounds. 'I must see this girl first before we can decide what to do. Obviously she has hidden potential unless she's one of those dazzling nurses who was able to turn the old man's head, but I can't see that, can you?'

'Oh, she's not dazzling, she's just a hoyden,' Coraleen said, and failed to notice a flair of interest quickening in Quentin's eyes. He was so used to girls of Coraleen's type, beautifully turned out with a predictable line in conversation, and greedy little hands, grasping intentions, eyes that said things that led down a certain track, and he was so bored with it. If this Beth Kennington was at all different from Coraleen's type he might make the effort to do something.

'Do you know anything about her family?' he asked.

Coraleen had to admit that she didn't. 'All I know is that she's been pestering Adam to give her private lessons and he is!'

'Good heavens, does your uncle know that?'

'Oh, no. Good gracious, no, he'd kick Adam out if he did, and that isn't what I want.'

Quentin was amused. 'Adam being the latest in a long, long line of men friends, is that it?'

'Not necessarily permanent,' she nodded, looking at him and waiting for his reaction to that. But he was older than the last time.

He touched her cheek. 'Dear Coraleen,' he said. 'I've been through the mill and suffered once before. I have to think very carefully before I go on the old treadmill again, especially having regard to my connection with your uncle.' But there was that in his manner which told her that he wasn't entirely indifferent to her rather more mature charms. She had advanced quite a bit since he had last wasted a lot of time in her company. Yes, she had changed since those days. There was no doubt about it. A little harder, perhaps, but at least she was no longer naïve and playing at being sophisticated.

He was playing absently with one of her

hands and thought to turn it over and check the condition of the ring finger. It was bare as yet. She had been trying very hard to bring Adam up to buying an engagement ring but he was inclined to say that they were engaged, they knew it and what did it matter if other people didn't know it? He was hedging hard against needlessly buying an expensive ring just to give her the pleasure of flashing a diamond around. That was another thing about Adam which irritated Coraleen.

Quentin murmured, 'Odd, I thought I heard your uncle say that you were engaged to Harcourt.'

'Oh, yes, we're engaged,' she said bitterly. 'He hasn't got all that much money . . . not yet.'

'Well, for heaven's sake,' Quentin said rousingly, 'don't let's let him get his hands on it, if that's what you're thinking.'

Coraleen shrugged. 'Oh, he won't be the one to get Staddlecombe. He hasn't got any medical connections.'

Quentin did some thinking. 'Staddlecombe is the prize. I thought you said he was taking the trouble to give this nurse private driving lessons? Would that have any significance?'

Coraleen looked momentarily alarmed, then she laughed. 'Don't be silly, I told you. He's engaged to me. I imagine he's giving anyone private lessons merely to get them through the Test quickly and prove to uncle that he's so good, he can take on the new driving school when Uncle buys it. It's as simple as that.'

'You don't sound terribly pleased with things as they are,' Quentin remarked.

'Well, it's all very fine for you, Quentin. You're wealthy already. You're a manufacturing chemist, a terrifically good driver and actually you're almost home and dry.'

'Thank you for the almost,' he said.

'What's in your way?' she asked him bluntly.

'Dear Coraleen,' he said again, touching her cheek, 'you are not the type of girl who should ask blunt questions from gentlemen. You should work up to them, gradually, beautifully, cleverly, as you used to. You're just not trying.'

'Well, perhaps I'm not,' she said sweetly, 'but since you used to go out with me, I've got rather more clever at finding things out. I think I'll have to turn my talents to finding out a few things about you.'

'Don't waste your time on me, Coraleen. If you really want to do something useful, find out about Beth Kennington,' Quentin snapped.

*   *   *

Beth was so thrilled to get taken off the Men's

Ward and back to her dear women. They greeted her with open arms. Mrs. Gibbs, who had the lorry driver husband, said, 'Oh, there you are, duck! How's your driving getting on?' and Mrs. Tally whose son was on the laundry van said eagerly, 'I've been talking to my boy and he's got all sorts of good ideas to help you! You'll just have to be around when he comes to visit me. Ever so excited about it, he is!'

Mrs. Arky, whose husband drove a furniture van, said, 'As for my chap, he's no good at telling anyone anything,' she said in some disgust. 'But he did tell me to tell you that if you was to go and watch him backing a van through a small opening he'd give you a few points on how to back round a corner.'

'Oh!' Beth exclaimed, looking at them all with pure delight, 'you *are* dears, all of you, but you know, I've got a horrid feeling I'm not going to get through this Test.'

'Now don't talk like that,' they begged her. 'That's silly. You've got to get through it, now haven't you? Besides, there's bound to be a young man in it somewhere who'll be pleased!'

Beth pulled a face and thought of Howard, who lived so near yet who had slipped into this habit of writing a letter once a week when he wasn't free to see her. This habit was putting him more and more in the background so that he had become less of a real person than Adam. Sometimes she could hardly remember what Howard looked like except that his eyes were so very serious and earnest behind those glasses of his.

Sometimes the urge came over her to go to his office in her free time, and burst in on him and check that he still cared about her, but there were times when she was almost afraid to see him again for fear he would appear to have shrunk a little in stature because Adam was so big and inclined to blot everything and everybody else out. It was a dangerous viewpoint, yet she found herself living for the time every day when she was to go out with him in the car. It didn't matter how cross he got with her, she was with him and that was all that mattered, and though she was well aware that she shouldn't be letting this run on, she couldn't stop it.

That afternoon, Miss Frisby was admitted to the ward. It was a shock at first to Beth, who had been in the sluice at the time. But when Beth heard that it was only because of Miss Frisby's rheumatism, it seemed a sensible thing for Miss Frisby to agree to have treatment. But a new problem appeared. It upset her niece Rose so much, and Beth was detailed to sit by Rose and talk to her about it.

Rose said wildly, 'It was an empty bed and then all of a sudden I saw my aunt being brought in. She must have had a heart attack—they wouldn't just bring her in because of her rheumatism.'

Considering that Rose was a teacher and normally quite cool and calm, it seemed odd to Beth. She decided there must be a great bond between these two women, and she warmed to Rose. 'Dear Miss Carver,' she smiled, 'you must know your aunt wouldn't be in this ward if she'd had a heart attack, she'd be in the Cardiac section.'

'Then she must have had a fall!' Rose fretted.

'Well, if she did, it would be through her rheumatism. She told me only the other day what a trial all movement was becoming and if anything can be done to alleviate it, isn't that sense? Besides, now you're in here, there isn't anyone to look after her.' Beth searched around in her mind for other benefits, and remembered to say, 'She might even get well enough to drive about again. She'd like that, I know.'

Rose brightened up at that, and inevitably remembered Beth's problem. 'But that would be marvellous! If she's able to drive again, persuade her to go out with you and give you some help. She's a very good driver, really she is,' and Beth sat there for the rest of the fifteen minutes she had been allowed, regaling Rose with the dreadful things she did during her driving lessons, and without really realising it, betrayed that the instructor was young and handsome and had given up time of his own—meal times—to help Beth. Rose considered privately that if a young man of his size went willingly without food in order to teach Beth to drive, then he must be either a very devoted teacher of the school or in love with Beth. But tempted as she might be to hint at this, Beth had no more time to sit talking. Rose watched her hurrying around the ward, until she reached Miss Frisby's bed.

Miss Frisby, while delighted that something could be done for her pains and stiffness, was agitated because she had been taken away before arrangements could be made about the cottage. 'The little animals—and I've left food there. It will go bad. You know how it is—they said there was one bed free and it ought to be snapped up while the going was good, and I just couldn't think. It put me off my stroke.'

'What about neighbours?' Beth said.

'But my neighbours are elderly, too, dear. Much older than I am and not very well. I can hardly worry them,' so Beth broke in, 'I know, you'd like me to go and see to it for you, would you?' and Miss Frisby looked so pleased and relieved that Beth was glad she had made the suggestion, although that might mean losing one driving lesson. 'But how will you get there, dear?' Miss Frisby fretted, thinking.

'Bike,' Beth said comfortably, well aware that it wasn't fit to use, and seldom where it could be found. 'Or someone might give me a lift.'

But in the event it wasn't as fortunate as Beth had anticipated, as Jonathan Seagrave was the one who drove her to the cottage.

He had been going towards the Nurses' Home to find Beth. He had taken the trouble to find out that she had got time off and he began with a bland smile, 'Remember, I offered to take you out?'

Beth reminded him severely, 'Yes, sir, but you said in the little car, to let me drive, or have you altered your mind about this one,' she added doubtfully eyeing the sleek length of his newish limousine.

That made him laugh. 'Indeed I haven't. Nobody, but nobody, touches this baby—it cost too much. And besides, I love it too much.'

Beth got in, with resignation, and said she'd been intending to go to Miss Frisby's cottage, and detailed why.

It was a day when Adam wasn't able to fit her in at all until after dark and Beth just didn't think. So far as she was concerned, it was a patient who wanted something done and here was a consultant ready to take her, and to Beth he was just another car driver and here was transport. In she got, and Jonathan Seagrave had a wonderful time talking to her about how she'd been getting on and the things that happened on the ward. She delighted him with her pithy comments on everything.

'Tell me again about the old man,' he commented. 'Weren't you surprised that you should be named as a contender to his Estate?' so she agreed that she had been very surprised.

'But patients do do that sort of thing sometimes, you know,' she explained kindly.

'But did you ever expect that to happen to you?'

She pulled a funny face which made him laugh outright. 'I never expect things to happen to me,' she exploded, 'because I know jolly well that they always just happen and there's always trouble. But to be honest,' she said sobering suddenly, 'I don't think I shall get Staddlecombe.'

'You sound as though you really care about that mansion.'

'Well, I do,' she reluctantly agreed. 'It's a beautiful house. Do you know it?'

He had to admit that he didn't. Well, that was to say, he'd seen it, he'd heard it spoken of but he'd never been inside.

'Well, no, neither have I,' she said. 'But I used to be detailed to talk to the old man, and he used to talk to me about his home. He wasn't much good at describing things, but there seemed to be a marvellous circular staircase made of marble with very slender wrought iron banisters leading up to a circular gallery and the hall is circular and the whole of it is lit with daylight coming in a dome thing up in the ceiling right at the top of the house. Super!'

He choked a little over that description because he happened to know something about that light in the roof of Staddlecombe. It was in the guide book. It was an ornate double dome of glass, imported from Italy, especially made back in the Middle Ages for this house and it was one of the wonders of it. If it ever was turned into a stately home and thrown open to the public that was surely one of the things that would draw the crowds.

He said gravely to Beth, 'I get your meaning, and you think you'd like to live in a house like that?'

'Oh, golly, no, I never thought of *living* in it,' she said, 'and yet I suppose I would, wouldn't I? I mean, I would have to.'

'Well, I don't know whether there's any stipulation that it can't be sold, is there?'

'Well, I don't know,' she had to admit with engaging nonchalance.

'Don't you know anything about this, young woman? A possible event that could change your life, if you became the successfull contender for this inheritance, and you haven't made any plans,' he said severely.

'Well, I was only told by the solicitor how

it affected me as a contender. What I would have to do, which was chiefly the Driving Test. I'm all right for the medical stipulation, being a nurse, and of course Howard would run the Estate, being a solicitor and . . . oh, golly, yes. I forgot that! We'd have to keep the house in that case. Perhaps there *is* a stipulation that you can't sell it.'

'Oh, dear, *now* what have you thought of?' he asked.

'I was thinking about my family,' she said in a small voice.

'Oh, yes, that family. We never did get round to discussing that, did we? Is it a mother and a father?'

She looked at him. Those brilliant blue eyes told him she didn't like being forced into giving confidences and he was intelligent enough to see that. So when he said to her, 'Little Beth, I'm not prying. If you don't want to tell me about your family, don't, but you looked to me as if you'd love to have someone to pour it all out to, that's all,' she looked doubtfully at him, still unsure. 'I don't want to know. Let's talk about something else,' he insisted, thereby taking away the prop he had offered, and she felt curiously alone and forlorn and more than ready to pour all her family troubles out to him.

She had just come to this point and had drawn a deep breath to start confiding in him, when they reached the cottage. 'Don't you think it would be a thumping good idea if we both went in and while you're having a look round I'd demonstrate how I can make a really good cup of tea? Now don't look at me like that! I can, you know!'

'I'll take you up on that,' she grinned, 'because I'd love a cup and you really wouldn't like the tea I make.'

He followed her into the cottage, picked her up and dusted her down after Ben, the dog, had knocked her over, and decided he would take the animal to a friend of his until Miss Frisby went home again. 'She won't be in hopsital long, so this chap won't have time to wear out his welcome.'

Beth went round closing windows, turning out food and the bird in the cage, to take down the road to some elderly neighbours, while Jonathan—as good as his word—happily pottered around and made a good pot of tea. He and Beth settled in the cosy kitchen, and she poured the tea into the colourful mugs, and found home-made biscuits in a jar in the larder. Miss Frisby was an excellent cook and Beth, like most nurses, was always hungry and ate solidly while she told Jonathan about her family.

'My father's dead, you know. He was the second husband my mother had. She's been married three times actually, and my half brother Don . . . his father was the first

111

husband. There are lots of others in the family.'

Jonathan gave a good imitation of a man with his head being spun round so she said consideringly, biscuit poised in mid-air, 'I'm not telling it very well, am I? But actually, you see, my mother's always worried because there's not really enough money . . .'

'That's unusual, isn't it?' he teased.

'Oh, don't be silly. You see, she used to be comfortably off only there are relations left over from other marriages who are always in trouble. For instance, there's Isabel who never really earns enough. She's the niece of my second stepfather. It's very complicated, isn't it?'

'Very,' he agreed. 'What is this Isabel like? Let us pause to consider her,' so Beth interpolated eagerly, 'Would you like to see a picture of her?' He said he would, so she got out, not without difficulty from a bulging and overloaded handbag, a rather battered snap-shot of a plump, happy-go-lucky young woman with no possible likeness to Beth, from which he deduced that this was merely a relative by marriage. Easy to see what Beth had been trying to convey; that Isabel was surprised if people didn't care for her borrowing ways, especially if she forgot to ask first. A cheerful person who has nothing to call her own. 'What does she do?' he asked curiously, trying to pin a career on Isabel, but of course, Isabel had never studied for any career.

'She's not terribly well-trained for anything,' Beth said kindly. 'But she's very willing. She'll take any sort of job—serving behind a counter, in a store or bookshop, but she gets unahppy in a job if she has to stay long and she just leaves, which is very trying for Mother because then my mother has to keep her till she can bring herself to get a job.'

'I don't see why,' Jonathan said, 'If she isn't really a relative.'

'Oh, well, my mother's like that. She adores people to be around and she feels she owes them loyalty and she couldn't possibly give up anybody that any one of her three husbands liked.'

'Where's the third husband?' Jonathan asked comically.

'Oh, he died.'

'And where does your mother live?'

'In a house provided by the first husband. They sort of gravitated to it afterwards. We've always lived there actually. In Larkbridge,' she explained, dreamily looking out of the window and eating biscuit after biscuit, and Jonathan got the impression of a full house, family gossip, comings and goings, careless comfort when money came in, slight panic when it wasn't available. People with something (but not too much) of the winning charm that was Beth's special asset.

'And . . . is there a man of the family to look after the women, apart from the half brother?'

'Oh, yes, my mother's brother. He's a clerk in a bank,' and Beth looked really troubled.

'What's the problem there, Beth?' Jonathan asked softly. 'Bored with his job?'

'Oh, no, he's terribly anxious to keep it because he thinks there's some sort of social standing attached to working in a bank. Poor Uncle Ewart, and he can't do sums. Personally I don't think it matters what a person does, so long as he's good at his job. That's Uncle Ewart's trouble,' she finished earnestly. 'It must be awful to be the only one on the staff who can't add up.'

'Oh, dear. I seem to think that you weren't very good at figures, either.'

'That's right,' she agreed. 'Family failing.'

'Well, so long as you don't forget to remember whose figures you're adding up . . .'

She didn't laugh as he had hoped she would. She sat there absently watching one of the cats trying to push her cap across the floor. It had fallen from her lap. The cat had an imaginary boxing match with it, and rolled over, clutching the cap itself, and then got up and stalked away with great dignity, leaving the worthless object behind. Beth leaned down and picked up the cap, and absently pulled off the cat's hairs, but it was plain that she was troubled.

'Beth, come back! You're miles away.'

She shrugged and laughed. 'Oh, just giving it too much thought, I suppose. Deep thinking doesn't really agree with me.'

He wasn't going to let her get away with that. 'Well, so here we are, with your mother and her brother, and your half brother, I think you said? What does he do?'

'He's a marvellous car-driver. He works at a Service Station. It's what he likes best, cars . . .'

'I see . . . Not married?'

'Oh, no, he's only about . . . well, not much older than I am. Well, yes, come to think of it, he's four years older.'

She seemed half surprised and Jonathan thought swiftly that Beth was obviously used to acting as the big sister and not the little sister.

'And then there's this charming Isabel?' he prompted Beth.

'Yes, and there's also Shirley,' she said, and pulled a face. 'Actually Shirley's a school teacher and she works very hard but she's not terribly happy because there's one boy in the class who stirs all the other kids up and they're always having scenes and she gets into trouble with the headmaster which is really rather a shame because she's terribly good with young children.'

'That the lot?' he asked, pulling a face. Beth nodded. 'Well, little Beth, what do you think you're going to do with this family if you inherit Staddlecombe?'

She said faintly, 'Well, I don't know. I can't really see myself inheriting it, but you know, it's a funny thing. I keep going past the house and having a look at it and it feels as if it's beckoning to me. If only I could go in and see what it looks like inside.'

'If I could get you an entrée, would you go with me?' he asked her. He hadn't the faintest idea how he was going to get in because he had only attended in one of the reception rooms, on that one previous occasion when he had been trying to persuade the old man to undergo a further operation after that car accident of his. It would make the third operation in a long line and old Maurice had made up his mind not to have any more surgery but to endure a life of discomfort in that wheel chair of his. Not a happy visit, nor one with time or opportunity to look at the place, and certainly not a social visit. Old Maurice had none of the niceties of manners. He didn't want to be cut about, he had said, and after that, it was a matter of getting rid of the surgeon as soon as he decently could. Right to his death, old Maurice wouldn't have that last operation which Jonathan had to privately admit might not have come off.

Beth broke into his thoughts. '*Could* you? I'd go with *anyone* to see inside that place,' which made him quirk his mouth in a rather wry smile.

'We'll see what we can do about it,' he promised her. 'Now, all this food stuff—I have got this right, haven't I? Miss Frisby wanted you to clear the larder out?'

'It's her last batch bake,' Beth explained. 'She knows we nurses are always hungry—she was one herself once,' and her face puckered up in that delightful smile that he couldn't tear his eyes away from.

He went laden to the car, and put the dog in the back too. But after she had finished tidying and closing the windows, he still hadn't come back so she looked out of the top window. Had the dog escaped?

Beth couldn't believe what she saw. Coraleen Drew's car was there beside Jonathan's and they were standing talking.

They were friends, of course: he had taken Coraleen on that tour of the ward, she recalled. But she couldn't fight down her anger. He must have expected Coraleen this morning but he had said nothing. Was Coraleen going to join them? But after a while, Coraleen seemed to be reluctantly getting in her car and going away, but Beth was ruffled. She shut up the cottage, gave a last look round, and went down to where he waited.

He looked at her and tilted up her chin. 'You were looking out of the window, weren't you?' so she nodded. 'What *have* you done, Beth to make that young woman dislike you so much?'

She shrugged. 'I don't even know her. She appears to dislike me being a pupil of the driving school, but I can't think why. Her uncle doesn't mind and it's his driving school.'

'Oh, well, you know best, but I'd be careful of her,' he shrugged. 'Now, let's think: you've still got time on your hands. I vote we go and enjoy the sea breezes. How about that?' but she wouldn't. She was worried, though she couldn't think why. Restlessly, she said, 'No. Thanks all the same. But I must get back, and you've got Ben to settle. I'll go and tell Miss Frisby what we've done, and there are loads of other things I've got to do before I go out driving tonight.'

She hadn't meant to say that. He raised his eyebrows. 'Tonight? *Can* you drive in the dark?'

'Well, I've got to try, haven't I? I mean, I've got to tackle all sorts of driving.'

'Who's taking you?' he inevitably asked.

She was clearly reluctant, but finally admitted: 'Actually, my instructor. He's giving me lessons out of his own time.'

'Is he, by Jove!' Jonathan murmured, and

he thought of what Coraleen had been suggesting, before Beth emerged from the cottage. 'When are you going to marry your solicitor, young woman? I did get that right—you *are* engaged, no?'

'Oh, well, yes—no—that is, it's sort of unofficial. Howard isn't going to get married for ages yet. He wants to settle down in the business and we're saving to get married, sort of thing. It's really rather dull, actually. I don't want to marry, anyway, before I pass my Finals, and that's at least another two years.'

'I see,' Jonathan mused. 'And does the fiancé know about the evening lessons with the instructor in his own time?'

Beth laughed. 'Goodness, old Howard wouldn't mind that. He'd be glad someone else was doing something useful for me. He can't . . . well, he wouldn't, even if he weren't so busy working, because he doesn't let anyone touch his precious car.'

'I see,' he murmured, and he studied her. Was she all that keen on this solicitor chap, he wondered? 'So you don't suppose he'd mind me taking you around? Wouldn't knock my block off or anything?'

The idea of Howard attempting to knock anyone's block off, finished Beth. She rolled up into choking helpless laughter and made Jonathan laugh too. He slipped an easy arm round her and said, 'Get in the car. You'll choke yourself. I was only funning. Come on.' But he asked himself as he drove her back to the hospital, how much in fun had that been? How much did he dislike the thought of this dry-as-dust young solicitor being engaged to this wonderful child? How much did he dislike the thought of that marriage looming? He reminded himself that he wasn't a marrying man. Or was he?

He glanced at Beth and though he slipped her an encouraging smile, his mind behind the smile was trying to conjure up what Beth would look like when not in that dreadful student nurse's uniform, or the sloppy casual clothes she affected off duty; Beth away from the drudgery of ward work, decently groomed and dressed, with the background of his mother's home behind her. He tried to think of it, but somehow the picture wouldn't materialise. But then, neither could he visualise Beth against the background of Staddlecombe. He had the absurd feeling that the first thing she would do was the highly sacriligious one of sliding down the bannister of the Grand Staircase, and he winced at the thought of it.

He was also pretty sure that there was something else about Beth that Coraleen didn't know about and wouldn't believe if she were told. He was quite sure that Beth regarded himself as no more than an uncle figure or big brother at most, squiring her around because she needed transport. Coraleen had suggested Beth was playing clever, keeping several men on a string. Sourly he remembered Coraleen's words, but he was dead certain that such a thought would never occur to Beth. He wondered what Beth would do if he kissed her; he knew, instantly, that it would be the last time he did that. She wouldn't give him another chance. She wouldn't go near him again, if he slipped in such a way.

He sighed, and drove her back to the hospital, and felt that he was surrendering her to this handsome young man he had seen in the driving school car.

*   *   *

Beth had got things to do, so she had told Jonathan, but they were not all that important. What she needed the respite for, was to think of her own feelings towards Adam, before she met him this evening, and to consider all the other things that were being said and done. Uneasily she thought about Coraleen's fortuitous appearance this morning. If it had been Adam and the school car, Beth might have understood. But what business was it of Coraleen's if Beth was taken somewhere by Jonathan? Poaching, as Jonathan had been Coraleen's friend first?

What Beth didn't appreciate was that

121

Coraleen made it her business to see that Howard knew about it. It took Beth by sharp surprise when Howard telephoned her just as she was going out to meet Adam that evening, and said he'd like to see her.

'But that's marvellous, Howard! I didn't think you could get away,' Beth squeaked. Her enthusiasm was so real that Howard was taken aback.

'This isn't to take you out. This is a matter of business.'

'Oh.' Beth's disappointment was crushing and obvious. 'Can it wait then? Or shall I cancel meeting my . . .'

Howard didn't let her finish. 'That's it, you see! You've got a date. I've had it drawn to my attention that you're not loyal to me. That you're going around with some other chap. I couldn't believe it but it seems I was wrong.'

Beth didn't know whether to laugh or be angry, he sounded so absurdly pompous. But the injustice of it stung her. 'You don't listen. You cut across me just now when I said, shall I cancel meeting my driving instructor for an evening lesson,' she pointed out heatedly.

Howard ignored that. He wasn't enjoying this, but he had been made to feel a bit of a fool. He knew he was no good with women, and his lack of the social graces had earned him a dressing down from his worldly grandfather who pointed out that a solicitor was better with them than without, and what had Howard got to make up for the lack of them? 'You deny that you've been out this afternoon with a consultant, and closeted alone with him in a remote cottage in a village?'

'Oh, Howard, don't be ridiculous,' Beth stormed, and then she went very quiet and still. In spite of his accusation sounding like a 19th century novel, it was in essence correct, and who else knew about it but Coraleen? Certainly Jonathan was not likely to have told Howard! 'We *had* to go to the cottage. It belonged to a patient who wanted the food taken away and the animals seen to,' Beth said, but her heart wasn't in the explanation. All she could think of was that Howard had listened to something he must have known was wickedly untrue. 'Who told you anyway?'

'Never mind how I heard. Is it true, or isn't it? Bearing in mind,' he said heavily, 'that there is a scandal clause in the late Maurice Unwin's Will. Quite apart from your disloyalty to me, I thought you wanted to inherit!'

It took Beth's breath away. But all she could think of was that he had listened to a stranger. Coraleen? And how? Did she know Howard? Or had he accidentally overheard something?

'I've done nothing to cause a breath of scandal,' she said angrily. 'But if people are going to maliciously gossip, then I don't know what might happen. Have you been talking to someone called Coraleen Drew? She was the only one who knew what we were doing.'

She knew him so well, she almost waited for the little gasp to show he had been caught out, and it came. Now he would try to bluff his way out by blustering, and he did. 'I don't want to hear you say anything about Miss Drew. She's the niece of a new client of ours and my grandfather and my father are most keen on getting the business of Mr. Mason so let us keep those names out of it. They're clients.'

Oh, so that's the way it is, Beth thought. 'When did you first meet these people, Howard,' she asked carefully.

He was so bothered, he couldn't think straight. There was no doubt about it, Beth was astonished by all this. Could it be true? But it must be. Why should anyone—a new client especially—blacken his own fiancée's name? Besides, she admitted going to that cottage alone with the chap. Anger flared in him. 'We're not discussing my clients, we're discussing what you do with other fellows in my absence. Did you or did you not go into an empty cottage with some chap and stay there?'

She lost her temper. The wild enlarging and misrepresenting of a simple incident sent common sense out of her head. 'Yes, I did.

But there was nothing bad about it. I've explained what happened. You should trust me but it seems you don't—you're listening to these new people. Well, you be jolly careful about them. I don't know why Coraleen Drew has got it in for me, but she has. She's been talking to other people about me behind my back. You take my advice: they're not nice people. Don't trust them.'

To criticise Howard or his clients was asking for trouble, she knew. Especially in this case, though Beth couldn't know that the trouble was he had accepted these clients in his father's absence and his grandfather, on his return from Scotland, hadn't been terribly pleased about it. Howard was tired of being the junior, with less respect accorded to him than the Managing Clerk, and when he found he was actually being sought out by someone with as much business potential as Oliver Mason, he had been rather thrilled and proud. Not just his first client but his first combine, for Oliver Mason had cleverly hinted that there was a lot of business to be done here.

The grandfather was inflamed. 'Can't you see, boy? They're using you. Giving you the small stuff for some reason. You won't get the big stuff. Why, you don't even know who's got the big stuff!' and the old man further cut down to size his grandson by saying sweepingly, 'Paul Ingram! That's who! And in case you don't know, he had the late Maurice Unwin's work. The lot! So now you know.'

Howard's face had whitened, remembering as he did, that Beth would know that. As a beneficiary under the Will, she would have been to Paul Ingram's office.

Remembering those things, Howard said, 'Never mind about giving me advice about my clients. Just answer my question, truthfully this time. Did you or did you not go out with this Seagrave chap?'

All the smothered resentment she had hardly realised existed against Howard for his bossy manner to her, his neglect of her for so long, and the vague longings that she couldn't thrust down, when she was with Adam Harcourt, made Beth answer wildly, 'Yes, I did. And in case Coraleen didn't tell you, he's a consultant in my hospital, and probably a better bet than you are, Howard, because he's the sort of chap who tells a girl when he likes her. And,' she added wildly for good measure, 'I daresay half the village knows what went on and will be sending anonymous information to you. If they don't think of it, Coraleen will brief them!'

It was a silly thing to say. She should have been there talking to him, letting him look into her eyes and see how honest she was. But it hurt her to think he had listened to someone like Coraleen and just ring Beth up on the telephone about it. It was important enough to merit a quiet talk in his car at least, if he had to question her at all. Not over the telephone!

Overcome with hurt and the futility of it all, she no longer cared what she said. But of course, the mood would change later and she would be sorry.

'If that's the way you feel about it,' Howard said, 'then I think you and I had better call the whole thing off. I shall write to you tonight.'

'Don't bother! If you can listen to that Coraleen Drew instead of me, then it's time it was all finished. I never thought it of you, Howard.'

She slammed the receiver back. Everyone must have heard, though all the doors were firmly shut. All except Grace's and she poked her head round it enquiringly.

Beth's face was working, but she controlled it with an effort. 'You heard all that!' she said from where she stood. 'There's trust for you!'

Before Grace could answer, the telephone rang again. Beth picked it up and was surprised to hear Howard's voice. Grace discreetly shut her door and didn't come out again. This was a really bad row.

Howard said, 'And please don't go around saying things about Miss Drew,' as if he hadn't had to ring up again. 'She did what she thought was her duty and she's the niece of

127

my new client.'

'Is that all you rang me up again for?' Beth demanded.

'It's very important to me,' Howard said. 'You don't realise. I've been thinking for some time that you don't take me or my work seriously but I must point that out. There it was the other night—I ought to have thought. They were talking about you then—'

Beth went very quiet. '*Who* were talking about me?'

All he could think of was that scene, when he had been so deeply embarrassed and hurt, round the dinner table at Oliver Mason's house. 'They were all laughing about you, making it seem as if you were having an affair with the driving instructor.'

Beth was so furious, she could hardly breathe. 'Why didn't you tell me that you were going to their house to dinner?' she demanded.

'Why should I have? They were new clients. You're never interested when I tell you about the business I engage in during the day.'

'If I was supposed to be going to be your wife, why wouldn't you talk to me about a new client? And anyway, business is all you ever *do* talk about—certainly not the things a girl *wants* to hear!'

'Beth, don't hedge. All I'm asking is that you don't tell other people all those things you were saying about Miss Drew.'

'Well, apparently you didn't mind them saying things about me! And while we're on the subject, this must have been going on for ages and you haven't told me about it. You only write to me once a week and don't bother to see me. Anybody would think you were miles away instead of only the other side of town. You could have seen me. You're the one who's been disloyal. You've been carrying on behind my back and now you have the cheek to break it off and I shall tell everybody what you've been doing and I shall tell everybody about Coraleen Drew.'

Now she had started, she couldn't stop, and she went on in spite of Howard trying to say something at the other end of the line. 'She's mean and sly and horrible,' Beth said. 'And she spies on people, and she isn't to be trusted an inch and . . . I wish you joy of her!' She slammed the phone down, really hard that time.

It was unfortunate that she was on the point of going out to a driving lesson. She couldn't think straight. She looked at her watch and thought it was the arranged time, so without waiting for food, she rushed into her mufti and tore out of the hospital and down the road, but Adam's car from the driving school wasn't there. She stared unbelievingly and as she was already upset, she stood there simmering and thinking, 'Just

129

wait till I see him! He's always on about me keeping him waiting,' but as she stood there, the Town Hall clock struck. Absently counting, she realised she was an hour too soon.

That didn't please her. There was nothing for it but to get some food, and all she could think of was the chip shop down a side street. It was a favourite 'take-away' for the nurses. Beth shot across the lane of traffic, narrowly missing a bicycle, and got to the other side to find a—by now—familiar car going along with Coraleen Drew at the wheel. Beth thought in exasperation, 'That girl must keep on my tail all the time! What's she doing here?' So she ignored Coraleen when she pulled up and called to her. Coraleen wasn't used to being ignored so she put her finger on the horn button and kept it there until Beth, red in the face and conscious of everyone turning to stare, turned and went back.

'What do you want? Haven't you done enough today?' Beth flared.

'But what have I done? I was just driving along minding my own business when you shot across the road and I thought you'd be under my wheels.'

Beth looked stormily at her. 'I think you're just dogging my footsteps all the time! What were you doing *by accident*, on your way through Pockling Parva this afternoon? That doesn't lead to anywhere; you *must* have gone there specially!'

Coraleen said, surprised, 'Of course I did. I was going to see the vicar. He's an old friend of ours,' and it was probably true, too, because a man in Oliver Mason's position would probably go out of his way to make friends with everybody from the point of view of business, Beth thought furiously.

'So you stopped outside Miss Frisby's cottage in order to contact the vicar,' she couldn't resist saying tartly.

'Oh, don't be catty. It doesn't suit you,' Coraleen drawled. 'You know what it is: it's this striving to get your Driving Test passed to inherit Staddlecombe, isn't it?'

Beth glowered at her. 'What do you know about that?'

Coraleen appeared amused. 'Plenty. I know who the other three contenders are, too. They're all related to the old man, as you would expect.'

In spite of herself, Beth was interested, but she wasn't going to ask Coraleen who they were.

Coraleen said sweetly, 'And the nearest relative of the lot—well, of course, you would know, I suppose—he'll have told you already since you're always going out in his car in the evenings—perhaps I shouldn't have bothered to tell you, only I thought for one awful moment that you didn't know and that you wanted to know.'

131

'What do you mean?' Beth stuttered, her voice rising.

'Oh! Don't tell me you didn't realise Adam Harcourt was one of the contenders? Yes! He's a cousin of the old man. Oh, but you must have known! I understand the old chap was a patient of yours in hospital. He would have told his favourite little nurse everything, surely!' and because Beth stood there looking at her in stupefaction, Coraleen looked nicely uncertain, rather rueful and shrugged saying, 'Oh, sorry! Perhaps I shouldn't have said that. Oh, forget all about it,' and drove on, calling over her shoulder, 'Careful how you cross the road.'

Beth was so livid, she could hardly give the order for her chips, and they tasted like sawdust. She stared at them and realised she had forgotten to ask for something to go with them. In the end she gave up the unequal task of trying to eat, and left the shop.

Adam! One of the contenders for Staddlecombe! She couldn't believe it. But Coraleen had been so casual about it that there was really no doubting it.

I ought of course to ask him, to make sure, Beth told herself fairly, but she was too angry. The way Adam had treated her, from the start—that arrogance of his, and he *knew* that she wanted to pass her Test for this special reason, and bless me, she thought, they had spoken about it, hadn't they, and she'd asked him if he knew the other contenders, and he'd said no. He'd lied to her! Well, of course, that finished it, where Beth was concerned; to tell an outright lie—that was too awful for words.

She stormed down the road towards the place where she was supposed to be meeting him, compiling angry speeches and ripping them to shreds at once in her mind; so furious she hardly knew what she was doing. It still wanted fifteen minutes to the time appointed, but he was there early, hoping that she might be able to get out early, to enable them to have a talk before the lesson began. The minute he saw her face, however, he knew there was trouble.

She looked more like a boy than a girl, storming along with that odd angry walk of hers; wearing slacks and a workmanlike jersey, her hair standing out in spikes as it did when the wind got at it. He didn't think she was going to do much good with her driving tonight.

He got out of the car, went round and held open her door for her. He wasn't entirely surprised when she began: 'I'm not coming with you tonight but I've a thing or two to say to you, just the same.'

'Then get in,' he said. 'This street is much too thickly populated for private conversation, or rows,' he added, and half pushed her into the seat beside the driver's.

133

Looking at her angry little face he decided that they'd better go a long way from the hospital, so that there was no possibility of any nurses seeing her, she'd never forgive him afterwards if some of her friends came up and asked who she'd been having a row with in the driving school car parked at the back of the hospital, so he drove out of town and along a quiet lane that was sweet scented in the dusk. Both the windows were down and for the time of year it wasn't too cold, and when he pulled up in a layby under some trees it didn't seem as if there was another car in the whole world but their own.

He turned to her. 'Right, here's my chin. Give me a thump on it for good measure for a start.'

She looked taken aback.

'Well,' he said, 'I'm pretty sure you're aching to hit somebody and why not me?'

'It's past funning time,' she said. 'I can stand a lot of things but one thing I cannot stand is people I think I can trust, and then I find I can't trust them.'

'Hey, wait a minute,' he protested. 'Who have you been talking to, and what am I supposed to have been untrustworthy over?'

'Remember the other day when we were talking about me wanting to pass my Test to inherit Staddlecombe?'

His lips twiched. He couldn't help it, for at that moment nothing seemed less likely but of

134

course it was regrettable and he hastily composed his face but she had noticed the amused quirk to his mouth. She burst out, 'It isn't funny! It means the whole world to me, but the whole point is, I asked you if you knew the other contenders and you lied. You said quite clearly, no, you didn't. And you did! You're one of them yourself!'

The smile died, even in his eyes, and they were cold as flint. Still she was shaken by that direct stare of his, but it wasn't the same. He was looking at her as though she was a stranger, somebody he didn't like very much. He said, 'Let's have a bit of truth about this: as I remember it, you asked me if I knew who the *others* were. Well, I don't. I only know that you are one and I am one. Satisfied?'

She flushed. 'But you didn't make that clear. You made me think that you didn't know who the others were.'

'Er—is it relative?' he asked, coldly.

'Yes, it jolly well is!' she fumed. 'What's the good of you saying you will help me get through my Test when you know I want to inherit Staddlecombe and you're a contender yourself?'

'There's not much I can do about it because I don't have to go through a Driving Test,' he pointed out. 'I went through it ages ago and passed the first time. But I doubt if I shall inherit Staddlecombe which ever way you look at it because I haven't got the other

135

qualifications.'

'Don't tell me that you've got scandal clinging to you,' she said bitterly, still doubting him.

'No, not that,' he agreed, 'but I haven't the requirements in the medical field and I'm afraid that I wouldn't know how to run a great estate like that, so you may think that you're fairly safe if I can only persuade you how to drive a car to get through your Test.'

'You still want to?' she asked in a small voice.

'Naturally. Nothing's changed so far as I know,' he said.

'What about what I just said?' she demanded belligerently.

'Well, let's say that I regard you as I did all along—as just a pupil.'

Something of the light died out of the day. She didn't know why. She questioned herself as to why she thought he would ever have regarded her as anything but a pupil, and a rather unrewarding pupil at that. But somehow the way he said it suggested that he didn't even like her. Well, why should he? He was engaged to Coraleen, wasn't he? He was going to marry Coraleen?

'Okay,' she said, shrugging. 'Let's start the lesson.'

'No,' he said. 'There are one or two things I want to say. You were so furious when you were coming along towards the car tonight.

Where had you been?'

'To the chip shop.'

'The chip shop,' he mused. 'That sounds innocuous enough. Might I ask where you gleaned this information about me?'

She looked at him. What was the use of telling him that Coraleen had said so? She shrugged. 'If I told you who had told me, you wouldn't believe it,' she said.

'Ah, well, now, perhaps I might at that,' he said. 'It wouldn't be Miss Drew, would it?'

Her eyes widened. 'Well, I wasn't going to say, because after all, you're her fiancé.'

'Did she say how she found out?' he asked carefully. 'Because as far as I know, nobody else knew except the solicitor.'

'No, she didn't say. Oh, I don't know,' Beth fretted. 'All of a sudden I don't like any of it and I don't think I'm going on with my driving.'

That stirred him to anger. 'She didn't suggest that you wouldn't pass, did she?'

'No, not exactly. Oh, well, she always looks at me as though I'll never be any good at anything. I don't know, I must be rather low tonight, probably because I didn't eat much. Home Sister warns us!' She turned to him. 'Nothing can touch me about my work at the hospital, you understand, but I must say I get terribly fed up about driving. It's just as if everybody's looking at me and saying, well, they can drive and I can't. Do you understand what I mean? It's the sort of thing everybody ought to be able to do and I hate it because I can't.'

He studied her animated young face for some minutes and she stirred restlessly under his scrutiny. 'Well, come on,' she burst out at last. 'Say what you're thinking.'

'I was just trying to see you fitting into Staddlecombe. Why does it mean so much to you?'

'You asked me that before.'

'I don't think I did. You sure you're not thinking of someone else?' and she flushed because of course she was. Jonathan Seagrave had asked her that, and she had told him all about her relatives.

'I can't tell you. You'll laugh.'

'Indeed I won't,' he assured her.

'Well, I've looked at it outside and it seems to beckon me.' And like Jonathan Seagrave he asked the inevitable question: 'What would you do if you did inherit Staddlecombe?'

'I don't know why people seem surprised that I should want that place,' she said, hardly noticing what she was saying, but he noticed and his eyebrows shot up. 'It's just a house, isn't it? A very big house, but there would be money to run it. But that old man, he was such an unhappy old man. There he was, pushing himself about in that invalid chair of his, with no hopes of getting out or

138

even seeing his grounds, and all he could think about was what he would do when he passed on. And how he would dispose of Staddlecombe. I think that's awful! I used to try and ask him about his relatives but he wouldn't tell me. All he wanted to do was to hear about mine, and he used to lie there in bed laughing when I used to tell him about my family.'

'You haven't favoured me with that information yet, have you?'

'No. We're talking about old Maurice and why I want Staddlecombe. He said to me one day "You're the sort of person who will grow up into a great lady". I know that's not true, but I didn't feel I wanted to laugh. It just sort of made me proud and thrilled to think that a man, any man—even an old man like him, a bitter, unhappy old man—should think that about me, and I thought, yes, perhaps when I'm really grown up and not just bumbling about being a student nurse and emptying bedpans and things, when I'm really grown up, I shall remember that, and if I've got Staddlecombe, it will make me six inches taller, because that house is like a person, someone who loves and trusts one. It's . . . *something*. You know what I mean? Oh, if I could only see the inside of it. I wonder if I ever will?'

'Why do you want to see the inside of it?'

'To see if it matches the outside,' she said

simply.

'Well, as Coraleen's insisted on you knowng that I'm a relative, let me point out that I have a right to go there, as such. That being the case, how would you like me to take you there to see it all?'

She turned round and looked at him, her face lighting up. It was, he thought, just as if there were lights behind it. Just as if a great powerful lamp had been turned on. No other girl that he knew could look like that. He couldn't take his eyes off it.

'Oh, *would* you take me?' she breathed. '*Could* you? Would you be *willing* to? Wouldn't anybody say you *shouldn't*?'

He just sat there smiling and shaking his head to all that, and nodding where appropriate. '*When?*' she breathed.

'Well,' he said, 'I don't think you're in much of a mood to drive tonight, so how about now?'

She looked crestfallen. 'But the lights won't be on.'

'Dear child, the housekeeper's in the place, acting as caretaker. Her name is Yardley. Dear old Norah. I daresay that if we could persuade her very nicely, she'd make us some absolutely super coffee and what she's been baking today. She's always baking. I don't know what happens to all the stuff she makes but I've never found her without freshly baked pies or cakes or something super.

140

Come on, let's go. It'll be a change,' he said, and somehow the mantle of depression rolled off him, as if, now he was away from the Driving School and going to Staddlecombe, he became light-hearted and gay and he drove easily to the house that coloured Beth's waking and sleeping thoughts.

He gentled the car into position and got out to push the iron gates open. Beth sat back and let out a long sigh as he got back in the car and drove through.

He looked at her rather tenderly, only she wasn't looking at him and didn't notice and he said, 'Well, little Nurse Kennington, we're going inside Staddlecombe. Hold your hat on!'

CHAPTER SIX

Beth, who had had a preconceived idea about what a housekeeper should look like, after reading the classics, was surprised to find that Norah Yardley was only in her late thirties, not fat and comfortable, and when she wasn't cooking (for which she wore a workmanlike white nylon overall) she wore a well-cut skirt and fine sweater. Her hair was styled in a modern cut and she wore discreet make-up. Beth didn't know whether she approved or not, or whether Norah approved of her. But there was no doubt about one thing: the housekeeper was delighted to see Adam.

'Oh, Mr. Adam, fancy seeing you!' she exclaimed. 'And who is this?'

'Ah, well, Norah, I don't know if you are in the secret of who the contenders to the Will are but this is one of them,' and before he could introduce Beth, Norah smiled broadly as if she knew all about it and said, 'Oh, I see. I thought so. It would be Nurse Kennington, wouldn't it?'

She turned to Adam. 'If you'd said you were bringing over the little nurse who gave the late master so many happy hours, I would have known at once. He used to talk to me about her,' and that just set the seal for a quite happy evening.

Looking back on it afterwards, Beth couldn't really sort out what she liked most. Going down in the vast kitchen regions and seeing what Norah had been baking, perhaps? There was still a tang of good cooking in the air, just as Adam had expected. And such a wild selection of pies and cakes and flans that even Adam was moved to exclaim: 'Good heavens, Norah, who's going to eat all these?'

She composedly reminded him of the baking she did for local affairs at the church. The late master wanted the tradition carried on, she said. 'For the cake stall, at the Sale of Work, this lot,' she amplified. 'What would I do if I couldn't cook and keep house as usual?' But she invited them to eat what they wanted, and Adam proved that he had an enormous appetite. Beth looked at him and thought, No wonder he's bad-tempered when he doesn't get anything to eat. Now she considered him quite a nice person, as she tucked in as well. She, too, had had very little food that day.

Yes, there was that to remember, and the rest of the house itself. First she had to look up at the glass dome, of which she had been talking only that day. The graceful, delicately wrought staircase. 'Oh,' she breathed, 'I can just see Victorian ladies coming down that staircase in their silks and satins. I bet they made a shee-shee noise when they moved,' and that made Adam laugh. He put a matey arm round her waist and they went upstairs together, to see what he called 'all the best views' out on the darkening grounds. 'It's a pity that it's not in the day-time. You'd be able to see the lake from here. Perhaps You'd like to come over in daylight, would you?'

'What are you going to use for time?' she asked saucily and he pulled a face too. 'I do get Sunday off,' he told her, and then he remembered Coraleen and his commitment there. Beth noticed, and guessed what had shadowed his face, but that was his affair. She was determined not to let it spoil the occasion for her. But it wasn't easy. It was almost as if Coraleen had thrust herself between them, forcing them apart. He thrust his hands into his pockets so that he shouldn't put his arm round Beth. With determination he showed her the rest of the place, but now he was just being a guide, or perhaps, nearer the truth, a reluctant member of the family.

But there was one thing that Beth remembered, quite sharply. She had asked to see the old man's bedroom. Old Maurice had talked to her so lovingly about it and had said that his room was the one with the best view in the whole house. There had been installed a small lift outside the door for him, so he was able to reach the ground floor easily, without destroying the beauty of the Grand Staircase by adding a moving seat belt arrangement for him.

The room was an extremely handsome one. Beth stood there pivotting round, and conscious of sharp disappointment. This wasn't Maurice Unwin. She remembered him as a little thin shrivelled man with no particular dignity nor pride of heritage that one would attribute to the owner of a place like Staddlecombe. She tried to imagine him in that giant fourposter bed with its majestic carved posts and its heavy elaborate drapes and tester which appeared to be hand-embroidered all over. An important bed, fit for a king, she thought whimsically. Little old Maurice Unwin, in that? Perhaps sitting up making that controversial Will?

144

What made him think *I'd* fit in here, she asked herself, staring glumly across the wide expanse of beautiful Aubusson carpet to where she could see herself in a long cheval mirror. The ends of her hair were sticking up as usual, her nose was shiny, and those blue eyes blazing with . . . what? Disappointment, dismay, Adam couldn't think. Certainly she wasn't happy any longer.

She marched across the room to look more closely at herself. There was a dark spot on her jersey—she couldn't think where she had picked that up—and her slacks weren't particularly presentable, her hands no longer clean. She put them behind her in an endearing gesture, and she started prowling round the room with her head down, thinking. She started scuffing the carpet and then jumped, as if someone had actually told her to stop. And all the time Adam stood where he was, watching her rather tenderly. But as his eyes followed her round the room, his glance alighted on a place where something should have been. He exclaimed suddenly, and Beth turned, startled, thinking she had done something wrong. 'What is it?'

'That's funny. There should have been a little cabinet on that table.'

Beth breathed again. 'Well, don't they move the smaller things when somebody . . . I mean, when . . . after . . .' She floundered miserably. 'Well, they have to take an inventory of everything, don't they?'

'They do indeed,' he agreed, and he rang for the housekeeper again. When she arrived, he said at once, 'Norah, what happened to my uncle's little cabinet?' and they could see she looked quite confidently at the place where Adam had expected it to be, and seeing the blank space she registered surprise and great dismay. It was, of course, her responsibility.

She said, 'It *was* there! It was there when . . . oh, let me think now. I can't think when it was there last. It certainly was when the old gentleman was here, right up to the last night, because I remembered coming in with his hot milk, and seeing him bending over it and scrabbling with it, (you know the way he used to when he couldn't find a pen or something in it?) and . . .'

Adam nodded. He remembered very well. 'We must find it,' he said firmly. 'You know why, don't you?'

'Oh, yes, Mr. Adam,' she said. 'it's . . . it must be . . . oh, dear it must be worth thousands. It's a treasure, isn't it?'

He said, 'It is, indeed.'

Beth broke in, puzzled, 'What was it, did you say?'

'It's a small cabinet. It was brought from the East originally, centuries ago. It has some very fine carving, lacquer, goldwork on it; inlaid in places with ivory and silver . . .'

'And ebony in places, too,' the housekeeper

put in. 'Anyway, it's the workmanship itself,' she explained to Beth, as if it were Beth's fault, somehow, that it was no longer there.

They all stared at each other in deepening anxiety, and Norah Yardley exclaimed, 'Oh, what am I standing here for? I must go and search around—it's probably only been put in another room. Goodness! You see, I don't do the cleaning of these rooms myself. I left it to the maids, the ones that we've always had, and when I'm not around, Ted Evans keeps an eye on them. He's very trustworthy.'

'Then let us question Ted Evans,' Adam said briskly, remembering the man servant his uncle had set such a store on, and who had not, apparently, been remembered in the Will.

'We can't. He went,' Norah said bleakly.

'Went where?' Adam asked sharply.

'He asked permission to go and I asked the solicitors and they said it was all right. He'd had bad news from his sister's home—only on the other side of Farmansworth, as far as I know. I suppose I can get in touch with him and ask him. I shall have to, won't I, if I can't find it. Oh, but of course I'll find it. I mean, who would take just that? There's nothing else missing. At least . . .' and uncertainly she hurried from the room.

When she came back, it was to report that that was the only thing missing. She appeared very distressed and puzzled.

'We must find it,' Adam said again. And Beth, standing there looking at first him and then the housekeeper, thought, this is like a milestone. Whatever this cabinet is, its being missing has frightened them. And nothing will ever be the same again.

*   *   *

With three weeks left to her Driving Test, Beth felt that the days were going by on wings. Each day appeared to precipitate a new crisis, if not in her own life, then on the wards. One day her mother telephoned her frantically.

'You must get leave and come home and talk to my brother Ewart,' she said, and when Lydia Whiterod referred to him in that fashion, then something was very wrong. When things weren't wrong, she said, 'your uncle', so Beth said, her heart in her mouth, 'Has he got the sack? Or is he ill?'

'No, he's not ill, and he hasn't got the sack yet but he will if someone can't do something to help him. It's a matter of twenty pounds and I just haven't got it.'

'Oh, Mother, you must have!' Beth gasped. She herself hadn't got that much either. 'What does he want it for?'

'He's threatening to take it from his float and put dummy notes in from the children's Post Office game in the attic. I can't think what's come over him. He doesn't drink or smoke or take girl-friends out and he's got masses of clothes—he can't want any more. No, it's just that he can't add up right and there it is.'

'But what's that got to do with twenty pounds?' Beth asked wildly, and was shocked to hear her mother crying at the other end of the line.

'I took twenty pounds out of his box in his drawer. I needed it to get a new perm and new shoes and nylons and I didn't think he'd notice till I got some money from Shirley only Shirley has stopped her money because she says she'll want it if she gets suspended which she will if there's just one more row over that Imberholt boy.'

Beth stood staring at the telephone. Her hand was shaking. How could a family like theirs go to pieces over a matter of twenty pounds? It was such a small sum to make such a big flap over. 'Look, I'll go and draw out the ten pounds I've got in the Post Office and see if I can borrow the rest,' Beth said desperately, 'only do stop crying and do warn the others not to need any cash at the moment, because I just haven't got any more.'

Her mother sniffed, and choked a little, then she said quite unaccountably, 'Are you sure you can't let me have all the twenty, Beth? Honestly, I don't know what you do with your money. It's all found and there are plenty of young men to take you out so it isn't as though . . . well, anyway, it's very sweet of you, dear. Oh, dear, where shall I find the other ten?'

Beth put the telephone down and tried to think. Just a little more time, three more weeks. Just at the moment the significance of Howard's defecting hadn't struck her. She was still aiming in a straight line for the target of her Driving Test pass. So she thought of ten pounds. Who could lend her that?

Grace would be as broke as she was, she was quite sure. But Frances? She went without thinking, to ask.

Frances was making up her face with elaborate care, which was a waste of time since nothing blotted out her freckles, so she washed all the make-up off and decided to concentrate on her eyes and hair. 'Do you think I'll do, Beth? Oh, it's you!' she said.

'Yes, *Beth*. Right the first time. *Now* what's the matter?'

'Nothing,' Frances said, going an unattractive pink. 'Did you want me for something?'

'I've got a pressing need to borrow ten pounds, or any number of pounds. Can you help?'

'Wh-at?' Frances squeaked. 'Don't be silly! Well, don't look at those two pound notes. I borrowed those myself, because I must have cash on me. He never has any,' and she went pinker.

'What's the matter with you?' Beth demanded. 'Who is this chap you're in such a flap about, anyway? If he doesn't have any money on him, don't go. He'll be borrowing from you next, like my half brother Don. Oh, help, that reminds me—he wanted a fiver not long ago. If he didn't get it he will come back to me, and I must—What's the matter with you, Frances?'

'No, he won't come back to you,' Frances mumbled. 'I lent it to him. Well, it's no good flying off the handle at me. He said he missed you and he was your half brother and you are my friend and, well, I can't resist that type.'

'You lent him money?' Beth was scandalised. 'Oh, I'm so ashamed. I'll make him give it back. I must. I can't have him owing my friends.'

'Doesn't matter. I said he needn't pay it back yet. He's taking me around in jolly nice cars so it works both ways. Besides, he is rather super,' Frances said, smiling broadly.

'You nitwit, he is not super and you are not to go out with him. He's dangerous! In cars, with girls, with money—anything.'

Frances got up. 'It's no use shouting at me. I'm going out with him and I can't lend you any cash. Go and ask down the end. Sanders is never hard up.'

Frances picked up her bag and gloves and

pushed Beth gently aside and went out. She left the pound notes behind but remembered them outside the door, shot back and picked them up. 'No use going without them,' she said.

That last remark did more to upset Beth than the thought of Frances going out with Don, anyway. It meant that in a very short while Frances had got to know Don very well indeed and was too dazzled to care or to heed warnings.

Three girls down the corridor lent Beth six pounds between them. There was nothing else she could do but to go to the Post Office, draw out her own ten pounds and get it over to her mother. How? No use waiting to post it, Beth thought. Better scrap her next meal, dash over by bus, then dash back from Larkbridge just in time to meet Adam.

As she was rushing down the road towards the Post Office, she ran into Grace. 'Where's the fire?' she asked. Nurses are noted for their wit.

Beth glowered. 'Got to draw out some cash. My mother needs it. I borrowed six pounds but couldn't raise the last four.'

'Hey, half time.' Grace hung on to her. 'Sure it's your mother and not that half brother of yours?'

Beth skidded to a halt. Such an idea hadn't occurred to her but it should have done. Don was quite likely to persuade his mother to ask

152

for money for herself, knowing Beth would refuse him. 'I never thought of that. Oh, I suppose you know about Frances going out with him. I've just had a row with her and she won't listen to me. She lends him money.'

'I know. I've tried to warn her off him. Sorry, Beth, but I've seen chaps like your half brother before.'

'Yes,' Beth stormed, 'and Frances didn't wait long enough for me to think how I could put it to her that he's around the wife of his boss half the time. No principles, our Don. Can't think why. He just believes he's right, no matter what other people say.'

'Want me to tell Frances? I will, if you like,' Grace offered.

'I wish you would,' Beth sighed. 'Got a lot on my plate.'

'Well, here's another pound, if it will help to chase the worry lines from your youthful brow.'

'Oh, Grace, I can't run you on the rocks. You've got to eat!'

'What about you?' Grace asked, and pushed the crumpled note into Beth's pocket.

Beth couldn't speak. Frances might be fun to be friends with but Grace was the reliable one, when one needed help. Beth started to run. She hadn't really had time to stop and talk, but what she had said, dinned in her head. Don and the boss's wife. One of these days, he would get thrown out of that job, if and when the boss found out. How would that stand up to the 'scandal' test in the Will.

Oh, she thought, I can't be worried by so many things. And who would know, anyway? I'm such small fry. Who would find out about me, that is, if Coraleen didn't find out first and put it around, but even then . . . Oh, no, Beth thought, I'm going too far, trying to give myself the willies.

She wouldn't have been so happy as she drew out her last ten pounds, and formed sentences of advice to her mother, how to raise the other three, if she could have heard Coraleen talking to Paul Ingram, the late Maurice Unwin's solicitor.

'I didn't want to worry you in the middle of the day but I'm so upset. I didn't know who to tell. I couldn't tell Uncle—he'll get an ulcer yet with his own problems. May I tell you?'

She had chosen wisely as to time. It was the sacred tea break when nobody was allowed to disturb Paul. Coraleen had had good luck, too. The telephone operator had left one line through to the boss's desk while she slipped out to make up her face, and Coraleen had got through to Paul on the instant. He pulled a face and sat down preparing to listen. After all, she would either be approaching him in the role of the wife of a contestant, or the niece of one. Either way he had to listen, because he still couldn't see that little Nurse

154

inheriting Staddlecombe. Much as he would have liked to see it.

'Take your back hair down,' he advised with a half smile. 'I have ten peaceful minutes to give you. What is it, money?'

Coraleen was shocked. 'No, thank goodness. No, it's one of your contenders to the late Maurice Unwin's Will. The scandal condition, to be exact.'

Now she had, as she well knew, Paul Ingram's complete attention, so she went on, as if too worried to know how to frame her words, 'I have hesitated before coming to you, because it isn't a thing one likes to—'

'Who?' Paul broke in. 'Which contender is it?'

'Well, it's the little nurse. Well, I wasn't going to say much at first—one likes to give people a run for their money, and she can't help having a most undesirable family who have no idea what belongs to them or to other people. But now it's come right home into my back yard; well, what I mean is, my engagement's broken because of her.'

'Tell me again. Start at the beginning.'

'Well, I know she looks a funny little oddity, a scarecrow at times, but the gentlemen seem to find something in her . . .'

Paul quite knew what she meant. He did himself. He wasn't looking so friendly now, if Coraleen could have known. 'Go on,' he invited.

'But it's a bit off when one's own fiancé starts creeping out at odd hours to give her buckshee driving lessons in the hope of getting her through that Test, and there isn't a hope, you know, because she's no idea about how to drive. I know—I had occasion to drive behind her one day.'

'But knowing all that, how come you let your engagement break up?' he asked softly. 'I'm not quite sure, you see, if that interferes with the scandal aspect.'

'Well, it does, because she keeps getting men in quiet corners and looks most surprised when a person suggests it isn't the thing. I mean, there was Jonathan Seagrave closeted with her in an empty cottage in Pockling Parva for a whole afternoon—ask the neighbours! They were revelling in it. I'm glad they're not my neighbours! And . . . well, one thing and another, and I only asked Adam to give her up, but the fact is, she's bewitched him. He wouldn't give her up, so there it was. Engagement broken. And I don't know what to do. If I tell my uncle (as I shall have to, since Adam works for him) then Adam will get the boot. My uncle will be livid.'

Paul's head was reeling. That nice little Nurse Kennington? Guilty of such things? She had a rather odd family, he had heard, but they were talking of Beth herself, not the family.

'But I thought she was engaged to some solicitor chap, what's his name? Old family firm, Quested, yes, that's it. Know them well. Young Howard, that's it. Solid as a rock. Fine match for the girl.'

'He's broken off with her,' Coraleen said. 'He'd heard about all this, and as you say, old family firm, and he's solid as a rock. He couldn't take it.'

'Well, that complicates things a bit, doesn't it,' he mused. 'All right, don't you worry. Leave it to me. I shall have to get some sort of enquiry agent going, I suppose. I didn't want to have to. Never mind, I'll see what we can do. I appreciate it that you didn't want the girl to risk losing her inheritance and if it's humanly possible . . .'

'Oh, I only want to see what's right,' Coraleen said hastily, wondering how she could have given such an impression. 'It's Adam I'm worrying about. Connected with her, he'll have *his* chances messed up one way or the other, won't he?'

'Could well be,' Paul agreed, an odd expression on his face.

'What shall I do . . . about telling my uncle, I mean.'

'Could I prevail on you to go on as if you were still engaged to him, while I think out something?' Paul asked smoothly.

He wasn't pleased as he replaced the receiver. How his hand was forced. He would have to start private enquiry agents working, a thing he had avoided so far, because of that cabinet being missing. In the ordinary way, with a treasure like that, he would have gone to the police. But the old man had had a pathological dislike of calling in the constabulary. Paul, in his own way, had hoped to trace the cabinet to some quite natural source. He had personally felt that someone, one of the maids perhaps, had accidentally scratched it or knocked a bit off it, and had been scared enough to hide it, so he had asked Mrs. Yardley to make gentle enquiries, assuring everyone that no blame would be attached to them if only the cabinet could be put back, under the cover of darkness. That was all that was wanted: the return of the cabinet, whose worth was priceless. Who could put a price on that quite truly hideous thing, Paul thought wryly?

Now this thing had come up. He wondered what the truth of the matter was. A quick guess suggested to him that Harcourt had become enamoured of Beth, after comparing her with his chilly fiancée, and who could blame him? And if Coraleen had been bossy with him he was quite likely to have lost his temper. That arrogant young man had surprised Paul very much by consenting to be engaged to Coraleen in the first place. And Beth herself? Paul couldn't see her playing fast and loose with some other girl's man, but you never knew. He sighed, and decided to put things in motion. His hands were tied. He had his late client's very odd Will to interpret and couldn't afford to follow his own nose all the way. But Beth Kennington, of all people guilty of raising a village's wagging tongues in a first-rate scandal, wanting Staddlecombe as much as that child did? Well, if she wanted it that badly, she would have to find some way round losing her solicitor fiancé, he thought wryly, and wondered if that fact had occurred to her.

It hadn't. She had a stormy scene with her mother, a few sharp words with her uncle, who insisted he needed three pounds more but wouldn't say why. She lost her patience with Isabel who came in just then, saying complaisantly that she couldn't find a job to suit her and that she had a lot of troubles, too, because of borrowing without permission a brooch from Shirley's dressing-table and had lost it.

'Shirley does make such a fuss,' Isabel said, sitting down to wait for her mother to bring her some tea. 'But I wish I knew the ethics of such a disaster so I can cut short her noise when she comes in. Am I in the wrong, would you say, Beth?'

'Of course you are,' Beth snorted. 'Why can't you ask yourself the simple question "Is it mine" before you pick the thing up. If it isn't yours, then leave it alone.'

'But I needed it,' Isabel said simply. 'It isn't my fault that I have such bad luck as to lose it. I wouldn't have lost it for worlds.'

There was the matter of Don, too. Beth said fiercely to her mother, 'Tell Don to leave my friends alone, mother. He's going out with one of the student nurses and if he cuts up, as he does sometimes, I'll lose that inheritance. Yes, it's all very fine, everyone throwing up a wail when I say that, but if you'd all think about it, all of the time, it might not happen.'

Lydia Whiterod recovered first. 'Beth, dear, you're very naughty, the way you tease us. Of course it won't fall through, whatever next? Now do be a sensible girl and take things more calmly, or we shall have you going sick just when your Driving Test is coming up and that would never do. Think of us, sweetie, and how we need that old house and all the lovely money that goes with it. Oh, to be able to shake the dust of this house off our feet.'

Beth opened her mouth to speak, and correct that erroneous impression, on the spot when she caught sight of the clock. 'Oh, no, is that right? Oh, I hope it's fast, otherwise I shall miss my bus. I must get it—I have a driving lesson tonight,' and she ran.

The clock at home was right, for once. She saw the back of her bus pulling out. She skidded to a halt, overcome by the realisation of what would happen now. Adam would arrive for the lesson, find her not there, wait and fume, and by the time she reached there (by way of the next bus) he would be too angry to take her out.

She was almost in tears of anger and misery, and in no mood to turn down anyone offering her a lift, so that when the big car purred to a halt beside her, she automatically opened the door without looking at the driver.

It was, of course, Jonathan Seagrave, but as he said, soundly dressing her down, it might have been anyone. 'Don't tell me you accept lifts without so much as seeing if you know the driver first, Nurse?'

'Oh, dear Mr. Seagrave, don't lecture me or I'll weep, I promise you. I've had such a rotten day and I've just lost my bus and my driving instructor will be waiting for me, and everything's going wrong and I don't know what to do.'

He noticed that her lips were wobbling so he said hastily, 'All right, don't bawl, there's a good girl. Just pay heed to what I've just said, and meanwhile I'll be a good chauffeur and just take you back to the hospital. Pity, I thought I was home and dry for taking you out to a meal and being amused for the rest of the evening.'

'I don't feel like amusing anyone,' she said forlornly.

'Don't tell me you've been jilted,' he said lightly, not really meaning it. She astonished him by saying. 'Yes, I have. How did you guess?'

'Heavens, what's the chap thinking of?' he muttered. 'You sure he meant it and wasn't just blowing off steam?' But Beth assured him it was meant.

'Tell me about what happened to upset you,' Jonathan commanded.

Beth sighed. 'Oh, it's a lot of boring detail. You know about my family—I told you. Well, they all want something.'

'Money,' he guessed, frowning. He didn't like the sound of that family at all. A definite drawback if one caught oneself thinking further about this delightful child.

'Well, not exactly. At least, I suppose it springs from that.' Beth frowned, trying to understand it herself. 'It wasn't like that before I went to the hospital.'

'What was it like?' he wanted to know.

'Fun, in those days. Uncle Ewart never seemed to be so worried at the bank and my half brother was much nicer when he was a schoolboy. So were Shirley and Isabel.' Then she dried up. She hadn't meant to admit as much to anyone, least of all this smooth surgeon who for some reason was taking a quite unseemly interest in her.

She turned on him. 'What are you being nice to me for?' and made him jump. He

162

looked startled then began to laugh.

'Oh, Beth, you do me good. *I* don't know why I'm being nice to you. You amuse me. It annoys Coraleen. I please myself what I do, and there are times when nobody but you can possibly lift me from the black mood that comes on me after I've lost a patient, or when I'm depressed living alone in Residents. Tell me, are you always going to be in love with the world of hospital, as seen from your angle, that of a nurse?'

'Oh, yes, I expect so,' she said, giving it thought. 'It upsets me when a patient dies, of course. But I don't feel it's a black mark against all of us—the doctors and nurses. I look at it this way. We do our best but people do have to die some time and people do have to get born, and if people didn't die there'd be too many being born and we'd get all cluttered up. It's a sort of thing going on all the time, if you see what I mean.'

'But how do you feel when it's a pretty young woman who dies, for instance, because one of us couldn't save you by surgery? Or a jolly kid like Peter, the kidney boy on F.11. How about that?'

'Oh, yes, I know, one does get attached to them. The trouble is I can't say exactly what I mean, but I have worked it out to suit me. If I hadn't, I wouldn't be able to go on. I mean, it might seem that I bumble about, dropping things, and I'm always either laughing or

163

losing my temper, but I can't see myself doing anything else than nursing because it's part of my life now.'

'Then how do you fit in the thought of inheriting the later Maurice Unwin's fortune and Staddlecombe?'

She gave that thought, too. 'Well, it's a thing I want, but don't really expect to get,' she explained carefully. 'I want Staddlecombe because I love the place and because it's solid and important and it means something. But even if I did get it, which I doubt now, I wouldn't want to stop being a nurse.'

'Did the late Maurice Unwin know that? About nursing coming first?'

'Of course. He used to question me a lot about that. He said once that he didn't believe me because it was only like wanting the drudgery that people below-stairs used to have, and nobody would want to be a servant all their lives. So I tried to tell him how much more to it there was than that. It was the day when I'd first had to insert the catheter. I described it. That wiped the smile off his face,' she said, laughing at the recollection. And then, remembering what he had looked like after his last breath, she sobered, at the pity of it all. His wealth had done him no good at all.

She sat silent the rest of the drive back. She thought most of the time of what Adam would be doing, sitting fuming in the car. He

164

would be in the most awful temper, she thought, and she didn't want to be with him when he was like that. Tonight she had no fight left. She wanted to be on friendly terms with him or not at all.

But at that moment Adam wasn't in the car but in a call box. He had remembered a message he should have relayed to Coraleen's uncle before he left. Coraleen answered the telephone, and reluctantly agreed to relay the message. Then she wanted to know where he was and why he couldn't come over himself with it.

'Because I'm working, Coraleen. Give the message to your uncle now, will you?'

'He's out,' she said indifferently. 'Are you giving that Kennington girl one of those buckshee lessons, because if you are, I shall feel obliged to tell Uncle. The school cars aren't for that, you know.'

He had often wondered just what he felt about Coraleen. At the start of their engagement, she could be very sweet, a quiet person to be with, and at times very entertaining, in her own way. But just lately she was tart all the time, and she was showing too much dislike for Beth Kennington, a girl Coraleen hardly knew. Suddenly he was weary of the whole situation and didn't want to talk to Coraleen any longer, and was unwise enough to say so.

Beth arrived and found the school car

locked and empty. She walked away, puzzled. He must be around somewhere. But he wasn't to be found. She didn't think to look in the callbox. Adam could see her and was intrigued at the sharp disappointment in her fresh young face when she found he wasn't waiting for her. Disappointed at losing her lesson? That alone?

He watched her walk smartly back to the Nurses' Home. Oh, dear, now she'd be in an awful rage. Coraleen, on the end of the line, said sharply: 'Adam! Are you still there? You're not even listening to me!'

'Yes, I am,' he told her. 'You just said you were asking yourself why you continued to be engaged to me. Coraleen why do you?'

'Yes, well, I'm glad you raised the point,' Coraleen snapped. 'I was wondering how to broach it, because you know if we split up Uncle will hardly want you around at the driving school. Well, if that's all you care about the job, there's not much point in mincing words, is there? I don't know why I keep on with you. If you'd ever gone to the trouble of buying me a ring, I'd throw it back at you, but you didn't . . .'

It took five whole minutes to bring that very unsatisfactory conversation to a close, but he did it, tidily, giving Coraleen the feeling that she had terminated their engagement. He walked to the Nurses' Home with the feeling that a load had rolled off his back. He was free as air. Now he could coach Beth, somehow, for her Driving Test, and answer to no one.

She saw him coming, and tugged on her thick jersey, as the night had started to get chilly. She didn't know why she was rushing down to meet him, but he didn't look cross and he was wanting to see her: he hadn't abandoned her in disgust.

'I'm sorry I was late,' she began impulsively, as she ran down the steps to where he had reached with those long strides of his. She broke off as he had started to say, 'I'm sorry I wasn't in the car, Beth, waiting for you.'

'Oh!' She started to laugh. Both of them apologising at once was something quite new. 'Where were you?'

'In a callbox,' he said. 'Making an important phone call.'

'Oh,' she said. That little word, when Beth said it, encircled a whole lot of unspoken words. It now told him she thought she knew who the phone call was to, and why, and that talking to Coraleen was sufficient justification for keeping Beth waiting for her lesson, expecially as it was a voluntary effort on his part.

'Don't say "oh" like that,' he said sternly. They had reached the car and he unlocked it and held open the door for her. 'I have to add that it was a momentous conversation in which Miss Drew broke her engagement with me. Although you may think that doesn't concern you, it does to the extent that I'm now free to coach you in my free time as much as I like, without having to explain my efforts to anyone else.'

Her face blazed delight at this news, and then she looked crestfallen again. 'Oh, it doesn't matter now, though,' she said with a shrug. 'I forgot. I need not bother you to take me out any more or try to teach me to drive.'

Patiently he leaned on the roof of the car and stared at her. 'What's that supposed to mean? Boy-friend cutting up rough over it?'

She shook her head. 'You know it's only because it's one of the conditions of the Will, me passing my Driving Test. But the other conditions had to be right, too. They all were, but now they're not.'

'Why? What's happened?'

'The running of the estate bit has gone. I was engaged to Howard Quested who is a solicitor. Now I'm not. He jilted me.'

CHAPTER SEVEN

As by mutual consent they both got in the car and stared at each other. 'When was this?' Adam asked gently.

She scowled out of the windscreen. 'Oh,

just before the last lesson. When I did so badly, I was furious.'

'Any use asking any more about it? I suppose you could say it's none of my business, but I'd like to know. I mean, the chap didn't mind me giving you extra lessons. That wasn't it, was it?'

'Not exactly. Only partly.' She shrugged. 'Oh, well, what's it matter? I'll tell you. He's got new clients. Coraleen's uncle and people he does business with. Howard got to hear all sorts of things about me and didn't bother to find out if they were true. Well, he sort of shouted at me over the telephone to deny them. It seems he believed Miss Drew.'

Adam's anger spilled over. 'Just what does she think she's—'

'Oh, don't get cross with her. I suppose it's my fault. I just don't think. If one of our surgeons offers me a lift, that's it. I go. I went to the cottage of one of our patients—she was worried. She asked me to. So I went. What's it matter? It was only to see to the animals. He came in with me. Why not? He's a nice man. He took the dog with him to leave it with someone he knew, instead of the kennels. We had tea and some buns I found there. But Howard put an awful interpretation on it.'

'The idiot! Just as if you'd put yourself on the wrong foot!'

'You don't think I would?'

'I darn well know you wouldn't. Besides, I'd see you didn't, if you belonged to me. I'd take you where you wanted to go, myself. I wouldn't give any other chap the chance,' he said briskly. 'Are you upset about Quested and all this? To the extent of not wanting to drive?'

She hesitated. 'I don't much want to drive. I mean, what's the use? I expect you know in your heart that I'd never pass, and now Howard's gone, why strive for it? No, what I'd rather do is to go to Staddlecombe again. Oh, but there, what's the use of that?'

He sat and thought about it. 'There's a lot about all this that I don't know. I've got a better idea. Let's scrap a driving lesson as you say, and go and have dinner somewhere and talk. First of all, though, we will drop into Staddlecombe and see if the housekeeper's found out anything else about the lost cabinet. I'd rather she found it than the solicitors, though we've had to tell them.'

Beth settled back. It was all rather odd being friendly with Adam, instead of being snapped at because she wasn't driving properly. Quite odd that there wasn't Coraleen Drew breathing down her neck, though Beth didn't think she'd let Adam really go, if she saw Beth out with him. But for the moment there was this evening. 'I have to be in by ten,' she warned him, and he nodded, too.

Staddlecombe this evening didn't seem such a marvellous place. Beth couldn't understand it. Adam said, 'I always did feel that there was a special spirit about this house. It may sound fanciful but if one was in a tense mood, it seemed that the house was slightly less benign. When one is happy and content the house seems to smile. Perhaps it's the ghosts of people who lived here before, looking at us and not liking what we're doing. Does that seem fanciful to you?'

'No! That was very near to what I was thinking and feeling, only I thought if I said it you might think it soppy. You seem such a practical person.'

'Not where Staddlecombe's concerned.'

'Do you wish it could be yours? Would you live here?'

'Of course I would,' he said in surprise. 'But there's no chance of that, and I think we both know it.'

'Who do you suppose will get it then?'

He laughed shortly. 'Your guess is as good as mine since we now know that the other two contenders are Coraleen's uncle and a chap called Quentin Burgess who is, besides being an excellent car driver, and (so far as I know) without a stain on his character, a manufacturing chemist. I imagine that would fill the bill, wouldn't you?'

'Let's go,' Beth said suddenly. 'If I have no hope of getting this house, I feel I'm trespassing here.'

'And yet the old chap made you one of the contenders.'

'Yes, I've often wondered about that, since I knew,' Beth admitted. 'I wish I knew why. Just his sense of fun, I expect. I mean, nobody in their wildest dreams would see my family in here, and they'd want to come, you know, if I did inherit. Well, it's natural of them to want to. But they wouldn't fit.'

There was hurt beneath the fierce tones in her voice. He took her chin and upturned it and searched her face. 'I wish I could feel I was going to be the lucky person inheriting Staddlecombe, and I wish . . .'

'What do you wish, Mr. Harcourt?'

'Adam,' he corrected mechanically, his thoughts far away.

'Might as well stick to Mr. Harcourt. I shan't be seeing you again,' she shrugged. 'Well, let's face it. My lessons have run out. No point in paying for any more, in the circumstances. Take me back to the hospital, will you? Staddlecombe's making me yearn for . . . all sorts of things I'm never likely to have.'

When he dropped her at the Nurses' Home, he said, 'I wish you'd reconsider your decision. No, don't shake your head. Think about it.'

'What can it matter to you, Mr. Harcourt?'

'Well, it does. Very much. And this isn't

the time or the place to tell you how. Do keep in touch, that's all.'

Beth was quite sure she wouldn't. In her heart she thought he would go back to Coraleen. He looked all odd without the pressure of that girl on his back. Beth wasn't used to his relaxed manner and it made her uneasy this evening.

She had other worries, too. There was a man always hanging about outside the Nurses' Home. She had noticed him the next day, and as the days went by without seeing anything of Adam (for Beth was far too proud to do as he asked about keeping in touch, without a purpose for it now) she went out more for those walks which Home Sister prescribed, to get fresh air. She felt better for it, she had to admit, until Mrs. Tally, now up and tottering along to the bathroom, had a look out of the window and mentioned the man. 'If I didn't know better, I'd say he was a private detective. Well, what else would he be waiting there for, reading a newspaper for hours on end?'

One of those remarks that stick in the mind when one is busy and come out later when one is relaxing. Beth looked curiously at the man as she went past him and for no reason her heart started to beat faster. At the end of the road she looked back and found he had left his post and put away his newspaper and was walking in leisurely fashion after her.

She forgot him. She had undertaken to do some shopping for the patients. Now there were no more driving lessons, she had nothing else to do. She turned again at the end of the street but she could see nothing of him, but later she saw him standing by the lifts in the local department store where she had been buying some knitting wool for Mrs. Arky.

Beth felt a little sick. Why should a private detective be watching her? She went in to the Powder Room and thought she had shaken him off, but later, outside the Post Office, she saw him again. Never looking at her, but always near. It was with relief when Adam pulled up in the empty School car and said, 'Get in.' She did, because it was no place to stop, and also because she was relieved to get away from that man.

'He's following me,' she muttered and told Adam about it.

'Well, that might well be,' he admitted. 'I wanted to see you—a rather odd thing happened after I left you the other night. At the house,' he began, obviously with difficulty, 'Mrs. Yardley said that a man had come, whose name was Imberholt.'

Beth turned sharply and looked at him. 'Imberholt? But—'

'Yes, I gather you knew of them. Actually he's the servant at my boss's house. He has a difficult small boy, who broke open the garage and tried to mess about with my car.'

'That small boy keeps making a riot in my cousin's class at school,' Beth said tautly. 'Still, if I telephone the solicitor to say I'm out of the running, they need not bother to keep watch on me, and my cousin need not be afraid to try to keep order.'

'No, that isn't the point,' Adam said, uncomfortably. 'Imberholt went to Staddlecombe to see if he could get a job there. He and his wife aren't very happy with Oliver Mason. Besides, there's been more trouble with the boy in your cousin's class and I gather Imberholt feels that someone might start blaming his boy, when this time it wasn't entirely the youngster to blame. He's a little wretch, of course, but . . .'

'I don't understand how all this concerns me.'

'Well, it does, and I'll come to that in a minute. Imberholt told Norah Yardley that they can't stay in a place where the niece of the boss incites their boy to start a riot in his class. That's not on.'

'Did she? But why would she do that?'

'Your guess is as good as mine. Imberholt feels that all his striving and his wife's, to make the boy see reason and stop making trouble among smaller boys, is not going to get them anywhere if Coraleen suggests to the boy that it's rather clever to make a riot and get the teacher into trouble.'

'She did that? I don't believe it!' Beth said. 'Oh, I don't like her, but to go so far . . .'

'She doesn't know you've decided not to drive any more. In that case, I suppose it might suggest to her a way to start the sort of unwelcome publicity to make a scandal and push you out of the running. What do you think?'

'Oh, no, I can't think . . .' Beth protested, trying to imagine it. 'No, it's going too far.'

'Well, it's what Imberholt said. Of course, nothing could be done to get him a job at Staddlecombe unless someone inherits. I wonder he didn't consider someone inheriting who would kick him out the minute they entered into possession. Coraleen's uncle, for instance.'

'Who did he think would inherit?' Beth asked, but Adam had only to look at her. There was no need to say.

'Well, tell everyone I'm out of the running,' she shrugged.

'I can't do that very well, because I had the express intention to beg you to be in the running again,' he pointed out.

'No.' She shook her head. 'No use. Even if this thing doesn't blow up in our faces (I haven't heard from my family recently but I'm pretty sure Shirley will be out of a job, after that last riot—she's been warned) well, the others will present the enemy with a ready-made scandal, on a plate. No, I can't tell you about what they're doing, but there it is. They don't think they're doing any wrong, but with a Will like this one, one has to be super impeccable.'

'I know, Beth. I did wonder if I could perhaps be introduced to your family, and talk to them. They're just being thoughtless as you say. And meantime, I would like you to take up driving again. Think of my side: it's a challenge, with someone like you. And it feels like a failure when you opt out. To please me, won't you persevere? I do so want to get you through that Test. Never mind the money. We'll see about those lessons. But do try, Beth!'

'And what about that man who was following me?'

'We don't know that he was. Anyhow, I am surprised the solicitors didn't put a private enquiry agent to work before now. I don't say to watch you, but certainly to find that cabinet, so the police aren't called in. Old Mr. Unwin was so afraid of police and newspaper publicity.'

'Oh, is that all?' Quite unaccountably Beth eased out, and after a while, she said, 'Okay. You're on! I'll take up driving again!'

'That's the stuff!' he approved. 'Now let's see what we can make of you!'

But because of her new decision, Beth started to go to bed extra early, so she didn't hear the rumpus down the corridor that night, nor the way it was hastily smothered when someone gave the word that Home Sister was on the way. Other hospitals might be following the new line and letting the young nurses have more leeway in their times, but not the Farmansworth General. The student nurses at least had to be in on time unless a late pass was procured. Frances Loxton's name was being softly bandied about the next day because she had been out without a pass.

'Who was the bloke?' Beth heard someone ask, and wasn't surprised when the speaker was hushed, for Beth could see Sister making her unyielding way to their table. She didn't realise that they were shushing each other so that Beth herself shouldn't hear. She decided to ask Grace or Frances what it was all about later.

The news that Frances had been almost caught out without a late pass, and that she had been with Beth's half brother came as a real shock to Beth. *'Don?* I don't believe it!' she said.

Grace, who had been the one to tell her, shrugged.

'I've thought all round it. I wasn't going to tell you. Then I thought you'd rather hear it from me than anyone else. What I thought was, you might tell your Don to leave her alone. She's got no sense. She's absolutely silly over him. What I mean is, perhaps you don't know . . . oh, well, perhaps I shouldn't have said anything after all.'

'Well, that's a fine thing, after you've said all that!' Beth exploded. 'Personally I wouldn't mind if Frances was the one to marry our Don, but I agree with you, someone ought to stop the silly clot from being out after hours. Don is a bit irresponsible. He is free to come and go as he likes but he ought to realise that we haven't got that freedom. Well, he does realise—he knows I've often had to forgo pleasures because of being in on time.'

Grace opened her mouth to say, who said anything about marriage. But then, she thought, as she hastily turned away without saying anything, you couldn't go too far with Beth. She did worship that odd family of hers so much, and it was really quite peculiar, for if Grace hadn't known the situation, she would have thought that there was no connection between Beth and that curious lot of people, who seemed to have no idea of right and wrong, and who just went straight through life pleasing themselves.

It wasn't any use saying anything after that day, Grace realised, for she was staggered by the news that Beth had altered her mind and was taking up her driving lessons again. It was so comforting to have someone like Adam having such faith in her, Beth felt, and as he was coaching her in his free time, and she wasn't involved in more outlay, she went into the thing with rather more than her usual enthusiasm. Adam was pleased with the result, too. It was as if, now they were both free of their respective partners, there was such a release of tension that both Beth and Adam blended together in spirit, and whatever he wanted her to do with that car, she seemed to be able to interpret and do.

'You'll pass all right, I think,' he said, one night with only a few days left before the Test. 'You're a good soul. You are trying so hard. Yes, I'm sure you'll pass.'

There were wings on Beth's heels when she left him, for at the last minute, as if on the absolute spur of the moment, he leaned forward and kissed her, very lightly indeed, on her lips. A butterfly kiss that she could scarcely believe had happened. And when she reached the hospital, it fled from her mind because of what had happened in her absence, and which her friends burst on her to relay before she could hear it from any other source.

'Have you heard?' they asked her first. 'There's been an accident!'

She looked at the speaker, but someone else said quickly, 'A car accident. The car's a write-off, and it was brand-new. A really plushy one.'

'Tell her who was in the accident,' an older nurse advised, in passing, so it was Grace who choked, 'It was Frances, Beth.'

'Frances?' Beth could only think of that freckly face and that gay girl who never looked on danger. 'Who was she with?' she forced herself to ask, as they stood looking at her.

'Your half brother Don,' someone said.

Beth's legs gave way. Wasn't it what she had been expecting all along, but had thrust the unwelcome thought to the back of her mind? Yet why should she have expected it? Don was such a good driver, even when he was showing off. But something wasn't quite right about the story. 'It couldn't have been my half brother,' she said in a little gasp. 'Not if it was a plushy new car. His car isn't plushy or new.' He couldn't have borrowed one from his service station where he worked, her thoughts clamoured. Oh, no, Don wouldn't be such a crass idiot.

She didn't know whose voice it was who spoke, but someone said, reather bleakly, 'No, it wasn't his. It was one he borrowed without permish. Actually, the one belonging to Jonathan Seagrave.'

★   ★   ★

Beth remembered that the town hall clock had been striking nine thirty when she had got in. She had been driving in the dusk and she and Adam had driven around for some

181

time after that, and he had tested her on her Highway Code, told her what to expect at the Test. And at that time Don and Frances must have been crashing somewhere. Beth shuddered as she thought about it.

She wasn't allowed to see either of them. Her mother was sent for, and she came in with her brother Ewart, and when Beth went towards them to greet them before they went up to the ward, the way they looked at her, as if they didn't recognise her at first, struck her like a blow. And as she looked at them, it felt as if they were strangers.

She sat down again, bewildered. Someone else had been detailed to take them up to the two side wards in which Frances and Don had been put. The nurses usually went into sick bay, when it was medical, but this was surgical. Frances had broken ribs and a fractured arm, and she was concussed, Beth had been told. Don had broken his collar bone and one leg. It might have been worse, she supposed dully.

She couldn't sleep, she couldn't eat. Everything had collapsed, because Frances had been caught out with Don. Beth didn't understand it. Other nurses went out with the relatives of their friends. What did it matter? And then she was sent for, to Matron's Office.

Beth had been there a few times before. Most student nurses got sent for at some time or other. Matron was a kindly person who sometimes sent for a nurse to have a helpful little talk with her, when the girl was homesick or doing badly at her work, or just not shaping up as she should. This was different. This was to tell Beth that Frances and Don had not only borrowed Jonathan Seagrave's car without permission, but that they had been to a nightclub strictly off the beaten track. A trendy new place that had already collected a bad name for itself.

Beth thought, as she reeled out of that room, that she had never felt quite like this before. Her head felt all numb and woolly. She couldn't think properly. She didn't remember much of what Matron said. She remembered more clearly a very dreary grey picture hanging on the wall behind Matron's head, of a bleak moorland swept in a storm, bare branches bent before the soughing wind. A very miserable picture that had made her feel lost and alone, especially as the chill day outside had started to become quietly insidiously wet. Two days before her Driving Test and this had to happen!

She remembered being asked why she thought that her half brother had imagined he could borrow a stranger's car with impunity and whether he had done such a thing before. She had wanted to say she didn't know anything about what her half brother did. He was a grown man and they had little in common. But that wasn't entirely true. Beth thought, with a sense of shame, that not so long ago Don had been getting much too friendly in a hole and corner sort of way with his boss's wife and that Beth herself had wondered why her mother and family hadn't been worried about that. At the very least, if the boss found out, Don could lose his job. Beth had the odd sort of feeling that he might have borrowed cash from the boss's wife, too. She was young and pretty and lonely and liked Don's sleek style and dark good looks.

Beth also remembered more about Jonathan Seagrave's face in the background than that of Matron.

Why hadn't he spoken for her? Why had he just sat there, looking at anything but at Beth's face. Beth had a hazy idea that Matron had asked her if she had told her brother he could borrow that car. Beth's voice wouldn't work. All she could do was to shake her head, but she thought with a kind of wretchedness that was tearing her apart, that the chances were that Don had seen her in that car and thought that what was good enough for his sister was good enough for him. But there was no point in saying so.

At last Beth, bewildered, had said, 'Are you . . . do you want me to leave then, Matron?' and Matron had told her icily that as such a thing had not been mentioned she didn't really see the connection. Beth didn't see the connection, either. She had rather expected that Matron would see her alone and would comfort her for the shock etc. Undoubtedly Matron was being bedevilled by Jonathan Seagrave, who was obviously livid about his car. Well, what did they think she could do?

She wanted Adam. She needed to tell him all about it, but she couldn't reach him on the telephone and she had been told not to leave the hospital grounds. She couldn't think why. She half wondered if they thought she had told Don he could borrow the car, but that wasn't sense, surely.

She went on to her ward the next day with mixed feelings and discovered that all the women knew about it. Mrs. Tally said, 'Don't mind, duck. It wasn't your fault and everyone knows it wasn't. Only they have to ask questions, see?'

'No, I don't see,' Beth frowned. 'I didn't even know they were going out together, and I still don't see why my brother had to take that car.'

'What about your Driving Test, then? Not taken it yet, have you?'

'No. It's two days time and they won't let me go out. I don't know why.'

'It'll be in case your best friend asks for you, I expect.'

Frances wasn't likely to do that. Her very large family were at the hospital visiting.

Beth tried again to get Adam and this time she succeeded but he sounded rather wintry, a long way away. 'Adam, I can't get out. It's not that I'm not bothering about practice and all that. It's something that's happened . . .'

Adam said, 'I can't talk now. I'll call you later,' and put the telephone down.

Beth felt crushed. It would be Coraleen standing beside him. He had gone back to her again. That was it!

Her work suffered. The ward sister had to scold her and the friendly Staff Nurse looked queerly at her. 'What's the matter with you, young Kennington?' she asked, with brisk kindness, when she came upon Beth in the sluice, her face wet, though Beth didn't know it.

'I have a Driving Test tomorrow and they won't let me go out.'

'Oh, is that all! Well, why didn't you ask for permission to go? You'd have got it for that, I should think! I'll see what I can do,' but she waited, as if she expected Beth to say something.

Beth said, 'I don't know why I'm in hot water. I didn't know anything about it!'

'Oh. Well, that wasn't what I heard,' the Staff Nurse commented. 'Mind you, I never did like the look of that woman, from the moment she came on to the ward with Mr. Seagrave, standing there in the mink, looking down her nose at the lot of us. Wish my

186

mother's dog had been there,' she murmured, half to herself. 'He'd have had it off her back. He hates fur coats!' and then she became aware of Beth's startled glance. 'I shouldn't have said that, young Kennington. Pretend you're suddenly deaf!'

'Yes, Staff, thank you Staff,' Beth gulped and felt suddenly better, and when it was time to go off duty, Sister said Beth might go to the driving school.

But it was pretty obvious to Beth that her enforced stay on hospital premises was Coraleen's doing. Somehow she had found something to blame Beth for, or to suggest that Beth had in some way been responsible.

But hadn't Coraleen done that all along? Why had she hated Beth so much? It was, to Beth, an unanswerable question. Coraleen didn't seem to want Adam, so it could hardly be jealousy. Or was it just a natural antipathy towards another of her own sex?

Something had happened to Adam, which convinced Beth that Coraleen had been at work here too. Adam said, 'Well, there's only time for one more lesson before tomorrow. I just hope you're up to it, after all the work I've put in.'

She looked curiously at him. 'My half brother has been in an accident with my best friend. It was a shock.'

Adam was silent, then he said briefly, 'I heard about the crash. Borrowed a consultant's car, I believe,' and then he told her to drive on.

It wasn't any use. All the warmth of his friendship had gone and he was as chilling as she had been led to believe any examiner would be. Her hands and feet wouldn't do what she wanted, and she drove so badly that he curtailed the lesson.

They came to a halt at last, and Beth could bear it no longer. 'For goodness sake, tell me what's the matter!' she cried.

'If you don't know, it isn't much use my saying anything.'

She gasped. 'What a feeble thing to say! No, I don't know. I don't know about a lot of things that have happened to me since I saw you last, but I do know this. The way you and I parted, I thought we were friends. I just ached to come and see you, tell you all about the things I've had happen to me, and hear what you had to say. I didn't expect to find you like this. At least tell me what I'm supposed to have done to you!'

He turned on her, his face taut and angry. 'Oh, give me the credit for not being a complete fool, Beth. Do you think a chap likes to hear the girl he's keen on is secretly running around with some consultant at her hospital?'

Now Beth began to see. 'Oh, Coraleen. It would be Jonathan Seagrave, I suppose. It's no good looking like that at me. I told you about him. He gave me a couple of lifts and Coraleen saw to it that everyone read something else in it. But I didn't think she'd be able to persuade you to see the wrong side of the story as she painted it. No, I am not running around with a consultant and if that's all you think of me, all the trust you have in me, then let's not bother with this stupid driving any more! I should have kept away from it when I packed it in before. Nothing's changed.'

She covered her mouth with her hand to still its trembling so she could say a few more things. 'I don't know what's happening to me,' she choked. 'To have Howard believe Coraleen and to hear him chucking me. To have Jonathan Seagrave sitting there in Matron's office, obviously believing I'd told my half brother he could borrow that car and crash it—and now you! Of all the lunatics around, I don't know which is the worst—Jonathan Seagrave or you. Both of you ought to have had a grain of sense and know that Coraleen *likes* to put bad things around about me (although *why*, I have yet to discover!) and you, of all people should know I'm not two-faced . . .' and then she broke down completely.

Adam pulled her into his arms and absently patted her head while he tried to think how it was that he had believed Coraleen's story, because he had overheard it. Yes, that was what had lent it authenticity. Coraleen hadn't been so clumsy as to go to him with the story. She had left the door ajar while she had been telling it to someone on the telephone. Who? He couldn't think, and it didn't seem to matter. He had been intended to hear that, he thought, his face flaming. His anger was partly against himself for being nasty to Beth about it, but mostly against Coraleen, because he was no match for her cunning.

At last Beth sat up and scrubbed at her face. 'Don't do that,' he said. 'Mop it. Here, let me,' and he took a clean hankie from his own pocket and tried to dry her face. It was blotched and red and her eyes looked sore with crying, and there was a spent look about her that tore at him. 'Okay, I need a few sound kicks where it hurts most, for believing bad things about you, but from where I'm sitting, the circumstantial evidence was pretty high piled and black. I wonder you let people do things to you, I really do. Oh, well, you can't help it, I suppose. You're a kind little soul, and they take advantage of you. And I love you, and I've got the push today and I've no job and nothing to offer you and I want my head searching for ever having listened to Coraleen in the first place and chucked my old job. No, I don't, though, because if I hadn't, I would never have met you.'

Beth was looking dazedly at him. All she wanted to hear was one part of a sentence several sentences back, which had sounded like 'I love you'. 'Would you mind repeating all that, Adam?'

'Oh, help, you don't really mean that!' he said, exasperated. 'Well, I'm not going to. I can't remember half I said, anyway, and I bet I wouldn't want to say it again. Oh, Beth, you must go back to your room and try and get some sleep. It's the Test tomorrow and you're early on. You'll have all the thick traffic, people going to work. Now remember all I told you . . .'

'No. No, I won't. I won't remember anything of tonight's lesson because you were horrid, and not like my friend at all.'

'I'm not your friend. I'm not anyone's friend. I'm so thin-skinned I only think of myself and if I'm hurt I turn to people and scratch and claw. No, I'm just the idiot who's got you under his skin, much good though it may do you.'

'Well, I like that much more than anything else you've said.'

'Would you hit me if I kissed you?' he asked thickly.

'Don't be a coward. Try it and see,' she said with a watery grin, so he did. It was a kiss that mingled desperation and unhappiness with jubilation and tenderness and something of fear, that this thing he had at last got within his reach might be removed from him. So many men had been interested in Beth, if Coraleen's story were to be believed. He shut his ears to Coraleen's voice, and concentrated on kissing Beth, till they both rose for air. 'No, my love, no more tears. Back to the hospital and get an early night. I'll call for you early. Oh, did you remember to ask for time off?' and of course, Beth hadn't. 'Shall I ask them, Beth? As your driving instructor?' but she wouldn't have that.

'No, I'll go and ask Home Sister. I expect it will be all right.'

'Well, don't forget you want to be out an hour before the Test, for a run around, to limber up. It's usual. You must!'

'All right,' Beth said breathlessly, and ran.

It wouldn't be all right, she knew. This was one thing she couldn't afford to be quite honest about or it would be refused out of hand, for to be out an hour before the Test, it meant that Beth would have go without her breakfast, and Home Sister wouldn't allow that.

She had just got into the Nurses' Home when she was sent for.

Not again, she thought in dismay. 'I did have permission to go out,' she reminded Home Sister.

'I know, my dear,' Home Sister said, with unusual kindness.

Beth stared. 'It's my half brother. He's worse?'

'No. Don't ask me. Just go over to Matron's Office would you? Don't stop to speak to anyone on the way. Go at once.'

Beth went across to the office where she had already spent such an unpleasant half hour, and her knees were shaking so she could hardly walk. She was sent straight in this time, instead of having to wait outside. Her heart was beating like a trapped bird. It must be someone dead, belonging to her, she thought. Nothing else could have necessitated this second call to the office.

This time Matron said kindly, 'You need not stand, Nurse. Sit down on that chair and relax,' so Beth knew it was to be bad news. Jonathan Seagrave wasn't there, either. Nobody was.

'Please tell me at once. Don't try to break the news,' Beth blurted out, doing the unforgivable thing in not waiting for Matron to speak first. 'I think broken news are worse than anything! It's my mother, isn't it? Something's happened to her!'

Matron looked taken aback. 'No, Mrs. Whiterod is perfectly all right,' she said firmly. 'And so, as far as I know, are the rest of her family.'

The odd phrasing was not lost on Beth, though she didn't understand it. Matron went on, 'The solicitor got into touch with me today. He wanted to tell you himself, but I believe you have a Driving Test tomorrow, so

I did rather want to wait until that was over. I remember only too well, taking my Driving Test,' she said, with what was for her a very human smile.

Beth was in no mood for kindness from anyone. Her mind was searching around, and she could only think of the scandal clause in the Will. All this effort, to be dashed the night before her Driving Test! This seemed to be confirmed when Matron went on,

'I believe you guessed that you were being followed or at least that a particular man seemed to be near you wherever you went. He was a private enquiry agent the solicitor was forced to employ, because of circumstances.'

'Because someone told him I'd been indiscreet,' Beth said bitterly. 'Well, I hadn't! It just looked like it to anyone who cared to read it that way!'

'You must let me finish, Nurse,' Matron reproved. 'The solicitor had to take this course, because of his late client's wishes. It also embraced, I believe, the very discreet search for a treasure from the big house, but that need not concern you. The thing is, the private enquiry agent discovered something about you, in the course of his enquiries, and of course it had to be reported to the solicitors.'

Beth whitened, and sat rigid in the chair. She might just as well have been standing.

She would have felt better, more normal. But Matron had said sit, and one did as Matron said. Now Matron began to tear down the fabric of Beth's life, to tell her she had no family, nobody belonging to her, ending with, 'I regret that things have a way of getting out in hospital, and I sincerely wanted to be the one to tell you this myself, not let you hear it from someone else. Now it need not interfere with anything, so far as I can see. This is your home until you have finished your training. Go and take that Driving Test tomorrow with a clear heart and tranquil mind.'

Beth looked at Matron as if she had gone mad. Clear heart? Tranquil mind? 'You really mean it's true, Matron, that my Mother is *not* my mother? But how can that be? I've always called her that—she's always *said*—'

'My dear, many people who adopt babies have the idea that it is kinder to keep the fact of adoption secret. I gather Mrs. Whiterod has a large heart and gathers in strays from all over the family . . .' She leaned forward, unconscious of the word she had used, but it struck at Beth like a blow. It was a physical pain, and she didn't really hear Matron saying, 'I think, from what the solicitor told me, that you might come to be glad that you have no relatives at all. That you are, in fact, on your own.' All Beth could think of was that the ground had been cut beneath her feet again. Once more, someone she had trusted had turned out to be a person she shouldn't have believed in.

CHAPTER EIGHT

Most of the women had gone home, who had expressed an interest in Beth's driving lesson. Only Mrs. Tally was left.

'You're not worried, duck, are you?' she asked, in concern.

Beth was finishing up before going off the ward. The Driving Test was the next morning and she felt too stunned to care one way or the other.

She shook her head and would have passed on but Mrs. Tally said urgently, 'Duck, whichever way it goes, come and tell me, will you, and to say goodbye, like. See, I'll be going home tomorrow. A bit sudden. Took us all by surprise, but they want the bed, and I've got a big family who can look after me while I rest up so it stands to reason, doesn't it?'

Beth came back and took the little woman's hands. 'Oh, Mrs. Tally, I shall miss you,' she said. 'All the others gone and all new faces. I don't think I shall stay here, you know.'

'Well, you won't have to, will you, once you pass that old Driving Test?' Mrs. Tally chuckled.

'I meant, if I didn't,' Beth amended that. 'I've got an odd miserable feeling inside me that I shall fail it and everything's gone wrong and I'm a bit tired of Farmansworth anyway. But I'll be in to see you tomorrow and to say goodbye.'

'Promise?'

'Promise,' Beth said, smiling brilliantly although she didn't feel like smiling.

As she had known, going out the next morning without breakfast was not a good idea. She was always hungry, and it made the waking feeling of emptiness ten times worse. It was a grey, sharp morning, unfriendly to say the least. Beth shivered. Well, it would be all right, she told herself, once she saw Adam's strong face and his straight gaze. He always seemed to put some back into her, no matter how low she felt. She just couldn't wait to reach the street behind the hospital.

But Adam wasn't in the car. It was someone she didn't know, until he introduced himself. 'Oliver Mason, at your service, my dear,' he smiled, and she disliked that smile on the spot. There was no warmth in it.

'Oh! Where's Adam? Is there anything wrong?'

'Not in the least!' Oliver Mason said heartily. 'Just that I felt for such an important occasion as this Driving Test will be for you, my dear, it merited the boss himself on duty, and not just an underling.'

She looked mulish. 'I'm used to Mr. Harcourt. He's been training me,' she said wrathfully. 'A change on the morning of the Test is upsetting.'

'Nonsense,' he said, coldly. 'Either you can drive or you can't. Now get in and let's see what you can do.' And as she still seemed far from happy, he explained further with a smoothness that set her further against him, 'You can hardly be surprised to find me here, when I learned that one of my drivers has been using one of the school cars and not charging for the lessons. Not particularly honest, would you say?'

'I paid for my lessons. Adam just gave me a bit of practice, in his own time,' Beth protested.

His silence was enough to make her feel utterly wretched. She started the car up but he stopped her. 'Cockpit drill first, I think.'

Beth had often said that a bad start was, in her case, fatal. She couldn't do a thing right in that first hour. Oliver Mason sat silently beside her, merely instructing her to turn left or right, reverse round a corner, make a hill start or turn in the road. Things that she could normally do very well for Adam she bungled, and not entirely because of this chilly stranger sitting critically beside her. She kept seeing the face of the person she had always looked on as her mother, and as such

198

had forgiven her for her selfishness, her continual coming to Beth for help with the others, and her cool assumption that they would all just naturally share Beth's fortune when she inherited.

Discovering that she was still in neutral, which explained why she couldn't start off at a junction on a sharp rise, Beth let out a stifled exclamation, still thinking that she could have freely forgiven all those things in her own mother, but that she couldn't forgive those things in a stranger, one who should have told her that she was merely adopted and not one of the family. That explained, she thought, why they all acted like Lydia Whiterod in one way or another; they had the right to say they were members of her family, either by blood tie or by marriage to someone close to her. Beth was just the cuckoo in the nest she told herself. No, that wasn't right, was it?

Oliver Mason's cold voice broke into her thoughts. 'If you don't concentrate any better in your nursing work, you could cause a grave injury to one of your patients. Or have you already come to the conclusion that you're not good at nursing either?'

She glared briefly at him but kept her comments to herself. The question, was it worthwhile going through this Test, was an easy affirmative, simply because Adam would want her to be a success. For his sake alone, she did try.

She tried when Oliver Mason abandoned her to a man who was just as chilly and negative. Adam had warned her that the examiner had to be like that. He wasn't allowed to talk or to explain, just to say what he wanted done. All the same, Beth, who had become used to the strength which flowed from Adam, and the confidence in her, however angry he might be at the time—missed it so much and felt she was doing worse every minute. She wasn't surprised to hear at the end of a gruelling half an hour that she hadn't passed, for she couldn't even remember what she had done wrong. Her mind had kept going off at a tangent, remembering the days gone by, when she had wondered what her father looked like, and had studied the photograph of Lydia Whiterod's second husband and couldn't find anything in that face to connect her to him. And now she knew why.

The Examiner left her in the car, and presently Oliver Mason rejoined her. 'Bad luck,' he said, and never did a greeting sound more false. Beth knew in her heart that he was glad she had failed. Well, why shouldn't he be, since he was one of the contenders. That moved him nearer to the top. Now it was Oliver Mason or Quentin Burgess. She wondered dully what Adam would say to her, or whether he would even know about her failure. Had he gone from this job already? For the first time she considered the thought that that might explain his non-appearance this morning. He may well have been dismissed on the spot.

Adam was waiting for her at the gate of the hospital. His own old car was there. Old in style, perhaps, but, Beth thought, with a swift interested glance at it, it looked lovingly polished and cared for. He followed her glance and grinned ruefully, and then he searched her glum little face and asked softly, 'No go, love?' and she couldn't answer. It almost finished her. 'Never mind,' he consoled her. 'Let's go and get something to eat. I bet you couldn't eat any breakfast. Oh, look here—' he said, in swift realisation, 'it's just occurred to me. I bet you didn't have breakfast!'

He marched her down the road and through an alleyway, past the shop where they got their fish and chips, to a little shop from which drifted delicious smells of frying bacon, sausages and tomatoes, and a great urn freshly polished, twinkled in the light of the watery sun that had just decided to come out. 'Tea,' Adam ordered. 'Hot and sweet and good. That's what you need.' And to the smiling fat woman behind the bar, he said, 'Just failed a Driving Test,' and her face dropped in ludicrous sympathy, before she began smiling again and pronounced, 'Then you shall have a real slap-up breakfast, duck, to put you right. You do look a bit peaky, come to think of it. Young people don't eat enough!'

Beth thought she could never look food in the face again but she ate that meal, and Adam ate heartily, too. 'I couldn't eat much first thing, for worrying,' he admitted. 'How did you get on with my late boss?'

'Oh, he did kick you out! Oh, Adam, and it was all my fault!'

'No. No, never say that love. He gave me a month's notice but I was so furious about him not letting me take you this morning that I just walked out on him. Doesn't matter. We're not wealthy but not hard-up either. I'll survive. Maybe I can get my old job back, for all I know.'

'What was it?' she asked, trying to concentrate.

'Research,' he said, but as her face lit with anticipation, he shook his head. 'No, no use whatever, where the will is concerned, because I was researching metal fatigue. Not what the late Maurice Unwin cared about at all.'

'Oh,' she said, her face falling again.

'Have some more tea, and perhaps you'd like to tell me about the Test, or have you had enough for one day?'

'I don't think I could remember much of it,' she confessed.

'Well, you won't get Staddlecombe,' he said, with a keen glance at her, 'but neither will that sponging family of yours. I expect you'll want to hit me but that really made me mad, the way they thought . . .'

'They're not my family,' she said flatly.

'Say that again?'

'They're not my family. Matron sent for me last night and told me what had been found out by the private enquiry agent. I'm only adopted. Nothing to do with them at all.'

Adam was furious. He couldn't think whether he was more furious at the way Beth had been told, or the timing of it just before her Driving Test, or the way the family had sponged on her, taken advantage of her utter good nature, knowing as they did that she had no connection with them and they had no claims on her. He tried to say so but could hardly stutter it out, he was so mad.

'Matron meant well. She was afraid it would get around and I wouldn't be told carefully. Anyway, it doesn't matter. It's just a bit queer, when you've thought of yourself as one of a big family and then you realise you're alone.'

'Well, that's just one thing that you're not!' he said roundly. 'Good heavens, I was going to marry you, even allowing for that awful family, but now they aren't a factor to be considered, there isn't any problem, that's if you'll consider marrying me, Beth, without a job. I think you don't really hate me, do you?'

She looked amazed at him. 'Is that a proposal?' she asked, and looked at the debris of their breakfast, the steamy atmosphere of this little eating place, the other customers in their dirty working clothes sitting around, and Adam, trying not to look embarrassed but with an absolutely adoring look in his eyes that even he could do nothing about hiding. 'Then I like it,' she announced with sudden satisfaction. 'It's the best sort of proposal any girl ever had,' she continued, her voice not quite steady and a tear rushing headlong down one hot cheek. 'And yes, I'll accept, before you change your mind, Adam.'

That made him laugh, though it was very emotional choky sort of laughter, she thought, and he turned in full view of everyone and kissed her.

There was a predictable roar from the workmen. Adam had forgotten for the moment where they were. He and Beth looked deeply embarrassed, and then they caught sight of the broad kindly smile on the face of the proprietress behind the urn, so Adam said, 'We just got engaged!' and as he pulled Beth to her feet to beat a hasty retreat from the shop, the men all started clapping and sending greetings for future happiness in their own way. 'Watch he don't make a habit of kissing girls in teashops, love!' and 'Keep him at home with some good cooking, if you want to keep him for good!' Beth turned and waved happily and scuttled from the shop in Adam's wake.

He drove them out of the town and they sat in his car in a quiet lane and cemented their engagement by a more private series of embraces, and Adam persuaded Beth to relax a little and stop minding so much about her disastrous Test that morning. 'I should have stopped you going through with it, I suppose,' he mused, 'but I knew how much you wanted to go on with it, and I confess I had no idea that Mason would step in like that. It was a rotten thing to do.'

'Don't say he made me fail, Adam. Only I myself did that.'

'All the same, for sheer psychological wizardry, it was the prize winner,' he said bitterly. 'I shouldn't wonder if Coraleen didn't think that up.'

'Never mind. What do we do now? Oh, I promised Matron I'd go back. Yes, I've just remembered—I promised little Mrs. Tally I'd go up to the ward and say goodbye to her. Oh, Adam, I'll have to ask you to drive me back right away. She'll be so disappointed if I don't.'

'Okay,' he said. 'But what then? When do you get free?'

'I don't know. Wait outside and I'll slip out and tell you,' she said.

Matron commiserated with her and said that she thought it might be a good idea from all points of view if Beth took the leave due to her now, and not waited the month that intervened. 'What with the disappointment of your Driving Test and the news it was my unhappy duty to give you last night, Nurse, I think perhaps you will appreciate a little holiday. Go to the sea. You look as if you need a good rest.'

Matron had no idea, Beth thought. What am I going to do for money? She thought of the money she had lent the family and a little thrill of fear shot through her. She would never see that again, she knew, and she owed Grace for some of it. She reached the hospital gate and leaned on it, and then remembered that she hadn't been up to the ward after all. Adam caught sight of her, so she stopped to tell him about her leave.

'How long, Beth? A week? More?'

'Three weeks, but what good is it?' She chewed her lip. No sense in hiding things from Adam now. 'I drew out my savings to lend to Mo . . . to Mrs. Whiterod, because her brother needed twenty pounds. Oh, I only had ten but I did borrow six from a friend of mine. I've just thought . . . I haven't anywhere to go when I get leave now. I used to go home.'

'Well, you can still do that, only it's a different home,' he said gently. 'Beth, remember—we're engaged to be married. What is the first thing you should do, and which you can now you've got leave?' And as she looked at him as if she were still stunned with the happenings of the recent twenty-four hours, he gave her a little shake and smilingly reminded her. 'Go and see my parents and family, of course, and guess what? It's by the sea.'

'Oh, I couldn't Adam. I haven't got anything decent to wear. I don't know your family. They might not like me.'

'We must give them a chance to find out, mustn't we?' He bent and kissed her quickly. 'Scoot and pack a bag and I'll be waiting.'

'I haven't said goodbye to Mrs. Tally yet.' But he wasn't listening. 'Beth, I've got such a good idea. Three whole weeks—can you sail? Right, I'll teach you. You can swim, I suppose. Well, that's something. And in between, we can employ ourselves looking for Ted Evans. Well, we'll have to do that somehow, love. We must find that cabinet and the enquiry agents don't seem to be having much luck.'

The cabinet. She had forgotten all about it. She went back and found Mrs. Tally sitting forlornly on the side of her bed, which had been stripped and was waiting to be washed and disinfected, after the usual method, before being remade for a new patient. The bed looked odd and Mrs. Tally looked unfamiliar in her street clothes. She clutched a carrier bag with her belongings in and her face was woebegone.

'Oh, duck, you came back,' she greeted Beth, her face lifting. 'How did you get on? Oh, lor, I can see you didn't pass. I've seen enough people come back from that sort of thing. They either look fed up like you are, or as if they'd been on the bottle. Oh, I am sorry, duck. What will you do now?'

Beth wanted to hug her engagement to Adam to herself as a precious secret just for a little while, so on the spur of the moment, she said, 'We've got to look for someone. A man called Ted Evans.' She didn't know why she had said that. There was no need to say his name, and it sounded rather silly, but Mrs. Tally, who was searching in her handbag for something, said, in a preoccupied way, 'Ted Evans. I know a Ted Evans. Servant at a big house, he was. Funny sort of chap. Thought a lot of himself because he lived and worked in that place. Talked posh when he remembered to. Didn't get on with his sister, though. She thought he was peculiar, wanting to be a servant these days.'

Beth caught her breath. 'Mrs. Tally, where did this Ted Evans live? I mean, it might be the one we want to find because he was a servant at a big house.'

'Well, he did live next door to us but his sister moved to the other side of

Farmansworth. She'd know where he is, I expect, because I remember them saying the old boss had died and they didn't know what was going to happen. That's always the way when you work for just one person in a place like that. Staddlecombe, that was the name of the big house. Oh, I've just thought! Isn't that the place you were talking about, duck?'

Beth nodded, and said, 'Dear Mrs. Tally, tell me where I can find his sister, because it's terribly important for Ted Evans himself.'

'He's not in any trouble, is he?' Mrs. Tally asked. Beth hesitated. If the man had stolen that cabinet, he was in very great trouble. She swallowed and said, 'It's to his benefit if we find him, of that I assure you. And you know I wouldn't tell you a lie, don't you?'

'That's good enough for me, dear. I'll scribble the address down. It's near the Bunch of Grapes in East Street, and she's got a lot of children and they all rush about and make a noise so I don't suppose you'll find Ted Evans there. Can't abide her lot, he can't.' And she wrote down the address on the back of an envelope.

Beth said goodbye and ran. It was their first breakthrough. She could hardly wait to tell Adam, for excitement.

She threw her belongings into her biggest case, and scribbled a note to leave for Grace, who was on duty at the moment. 'Failed Driving Test. Thrown out for leave and recuperation. Haven't forgotten six pounds. Will write you. Love, Beth.'

She wished she could have seen Grace. She would have liked to tell her about being no connection with Mrs. Whiterod and her family. Grace would be happy. She had never liked them, and had been very worried when Frances had been so infatuated with Don Jeffers. Frances . . . Beth wondered if they'd let her in to see Frances, but decided against it. Frances wouldn't want to see her because they had parted on unfriendly terms when Beth had tried to persuade her friend to break with such an unsuitable young man. Beth staggered down with her case and dumped it on the pavement and waited for Adam.

*   *   *

He was grinning broadly as he drove up. 'No regrets at the last moment?' he demanded, and as she shook her head, he said, 'What a relief, because I've been telephoning my mother about you and she's very excited and says of course you must stay all of your leave with us. She thought it was Coraleen at first and I think she was going to say that she was full up with visitors or that the spare room had the ceiling down or something. She didn't like Coraleen.'

Beth climbed into the car and listened to the bumping as he stowed her battered old case in the boot. Adam was a different person from the arrogant young man she had first known as a driving instructor. He glanced at her and said, 'Cheer up! It isn't decent for me to be so pleased with life and you're miserable. Would it help if I kissed you before we started off for home?'

'Before we start off for home? What a lovely thing to say to me,' she sighed, and gave herself up to enjoyment of his kiss.

'Can't be too long about it. It's rather populous just here, sweet,' he murmured, then kissed her again. He was a little light-headed, she thought, and grinned at him as he sat back with mock solemnity and adjusted his seat belt.

'Oh, no!' she suddenly exclaimed, startling him. 'What am I thinking of? I can't say I'll marry you and go to your home.'

'Why not, Beth?' he asked, going very still.

'*Because* . . . oh, Adam, we don't know who I am! I'm only adopted. Not even connected with a family like . . .'

'Hey, now don't start crying or you'll mess the day up. Beth, my love, never *mind*. I'm satisfied. Well, all right, let's give my mother a chance to say what she feels about it. Personally I think she'll be so pleased with you as a person, after Coraleen, that she won't care who your parents were!'

'No, no, it isn't the same. Please, Adam, let's just . . . did you tell her we were

211

engaged?'

'Well, no, actually I didn't. I said I was bringing someone home to stay—*not* Coraleen—and that it was a surprise I'd explain all about when I got there.'

'I'm glad,' Beth said shortly. 'I should have thought!'

'I'm not going to let you back out of it on a technicality like that. I only refrained from saying too much on the telephone, because my poor dear mother didn't even know I'd broken with Coraleen, and she'd naturally want to hear everything, and frankly I didn't have enough spare change for a long distance call of that length. Oh, come on, let's go, Beth, and don't be so glum, my love. It'll work out. First we must look up this Ted Evans or his sister.'

As Mrs. Tally had warned, there was so much of children's noise in the background that it was difficult to hear the voice of Ted Evans's sister. But clearly she wasn't trying to hide anything. 'He's in hospital,' she said at once. 'He's got chest trouble and to be frank, I can't look after him—I've got children. You can hear them! Besides, Ted was too ill to stay here with this racket. What did you want him for? Will I do?'

'Which hospital is he in, because we'd really rather we talked to him. I think he'd prefer it, too. It is rather personal,' Beth explained.

212

'Okay, suit yourself, but he wasn't up to talking the last time I saw him. If it's his insurance money, I know all about that.'

'No, it isn't. Which hospital?' Beth insisted, and was really surprised when Ted Evans's sister said, 'Farmansworth General.'

'My own hospital! I'm a nurse there, and I didn't know!'

But of course, with chest trouble, he would be in the Medical Wing. 'We've got to go back,' Beth said, replacing the receiver.

Adam didn't want to, but Beth was adamant.

'But it's still not lunch time. They won't let you see him until the afternoon, surely,' Adam protested.

'They might if I ask Matron first and say it's about the inheritance,' Beth said sturdily.

'I have the odd sort of feeling,' Adam remarked as they went back to the car, 'that though you're such a little scrap, you're going to get your way all through our married life. I wonder if I'm doing the right thing.'

'You'd better ask your mother,' Beth said cheekily.

As Beth had anticipated, they let them see Ted Evans. He was much better than when he had been admitted, and able to sit up, but he looked very upset when they were shown to his bedside.

'It's trouble, isn't it?' he began. 'About that cabinet. You'll be from the solicitor's office,'

213

he told Adam. And then he struggled to sit up. 'No, you're not! You're—it's Mr. Adam, isn't it? Haven't seen you since—'

'Since I shaved off the beard I had at university,' Adam grinned. 'Changes a person, doesn't it?'

They reminisced a bit, then Adam said, 'Now look, Evans, old chap, do you know what happened to my Uncle's cabinet? It's a long shot and we didn't want to come and bother you . . .'

Beth said, 'Anything at all that you remember would be useful,' and was staggered when he said to them both, 'Well, I've got it, haven't I?'

Adam looked completely taken aback. He had resolutely refused to believe that any old servant of his uncle could steal. Old Maurice Unwin was a shrewd assessor of people's characters. Had he slipped up at last?

He pulled the stool out from under the bed for himself, as Beth sat in the chair a nurse brought for her. 'Now look,' Adam said, 'it was only discovered missing the other day when I was at Staddlecombe with Miss Kennington here, who is another contender . . .'

'So this is Miss Kennington, the guvnor's little nurse! He was always talking about her.' He looked curiously at her. 'Yes, now I begin to see, miss. I wish I'd met you before.'

'Would it have made any difference?' Beth

asked unhappily, sure that the man had stolen the cabinet.

'No, I don't think so, miss. See, I've got the cabinet in my room at my sister's.'

They both looked aghast at him and at each other. 'I didn't steal it. Oh, look, sir, I'd better tell you from the beginning.'

'I think you'd better,' Adam said. 'In fact I think I'd better send for the solicitor to hear this,' but Beth, who understood patients very well, took his arm and said, 'No, let him tell it his own way, just for us,' and frowned at Adam. The chances were that the man would dry up in fear if Paul Ingram came in person.

'Okay, then,' Adam agreed. 'You just tell us in your own words. Take your time.'

'Well, see, it was this here Will. All them people in a sort of competition. The guvnor was lying there one night and there was me making up his fire after I'd got him undressed and into bed. Did that every night for him. He wouldn't let anyone else touch him. And suddenly he says to me, "What have I done, Ted?" He looked so upset, I dropped the poker and went over to the bed. I thought he'd ricked his poor back or something.

'"That Will of mine, Ted. Suppose I've made it easy for the wrong ones to inherit. Me and my clever Will-making".'

Beth stole a glance at Adam but Ted Evans wasn't looking at them. He was staring across the ward into the middle distance, no doubt remembering that last night with his old master. 'He kept on fretting about it. "I know which I *want* to inherit, but suppose it doesn't work out like that? Suppose there's dirty work? Suppose there's harm done to the right ones." Oh, he did keep on.'

'Yes, what else happened?' Beth prompted gently, taking his hand in hers.

'Well, near his end, the guvnor decided he must do something about it and send for his solicitor but he wasn't there. "I'm not going to last the night," he kept saying over and over. So I asked him why he didn't write down what was bothering him. Oh, that eased him a treat. He said why didn't he think of it before. So I gave him his writing things and held him up so he could put pen to paper, and he wrote out a proper document. You know, the guvnor fancied himself for his legal knowledge. Read up old cases like other folks read thrillers, he did.'

Adam began to get restive but Beth frowned at him.

'I sent for the doctor. I didn't like the looks of the guvnor, but the doctor was out at a confinement. Wouldn't you know it, only the locum was there. So when he came, the guvnor asked him and me to be the witnesses. "It's all right and tight," he said to us. "I've told 'em who I want to really have the place, Ted, but I'll put it away safely." And he made us turn our backs while he hid it. But I knew where he'd put it. We couldn't get the locum to go without giving the guvnor a sedative though or else the guvnor would have said more than he did, I'm sure. But when we were alone, the guvnor said, "I've hid it in the cabinet, Ted."'

'The cabinet!' Beth gasped.

Ted Evans nodded. 'Yes, he was a rare one for hiding things and they were usually in that ugly old piece of furniture because it had a secret catch and he felt his treasures were safe. "Ted", he says, "you get it out when the time comes, you being the only other one besides me who can work the secret catch." And then the dope worked. That flipping doctor! I never did get to ask the guvnor what the special instructions were or what he meant by when the time came. I suppose I should have told Mr. Ingram, but the guvnor didn't tell me to. And to tell you the truth it was all such confusion when the guvnor died that I forgot about it.'

'How could you forget such a trust that had been placed on you?' Adam asked sternly, but Beth touched his arm again. They still wanted to know a lot of things.

'Well, Mr. Adam, you know what Mr. Mason's like and Mr. Ingram was all over the place with his clerks, taking inventories and most of the time I didn't know where the cabinet was. Then I thought I'd better do something about it.' He looked glum, so Beth

217

squeezed his hand and said, 'Yes, and then what?'

Ted said, 'You'll never believe this but I couldn't get the secret catch to work. Either I'd forgotten the proper way to do it or someone else had been trying to open it or maybe it had just jammed. I don't know.'

'But why didn't you approach the solicitor then, man?' Adam demanded, impatiently.

'He was ill, Adam,' Beth said softly.

'That's right, miss. Didn't feel too good just then, and I'd got the thing in my room on account of folks kept interrupting—maids and the housekeeper and the clerks. I thought if I could just have a longish time with it, I'd make it work.'

'But you never did?'

'No, well, I bethought me of my sister and if I could get to her place I'd at least have a room to myself where I wouldn't be disturbed and I could take my time trying to open the thing. Only . . . well, I got this chest trouble and they whipped me off to hospital. Well, my sister couldn't look after me. Too busy. But I'm so worried—I made her promise faithfully those kids wouldn't get to the cabinet.'

'Oh, they won't, I'm sure,' Beth comforted him.

'But they might! You don't understand. Being so bright—all those colours and patterns—they don't understand it's old

218

Eastern lacquer and carving. They think it's—well, you'll never believe this but they thought it'd do fine for their play they're doing at school. Oh, I do hope my sister's kept her promise.'

They had to go then. In a way it was satisfactory, in that the cabinet was traced at last. But how would the solicitor view the thing? Evans had taken the cabinet away. Beth was as worried as Adam. The old man had thought a lot of Evans.

Back at his sister's house, it should have been plain sailing. 'Well, if you can prove that my brother said you could take the thing away, I'd be jolly glad,' she said, 'because those kids of mine have been on at me to let them have it for the school play ever since they saw it. It's an Eastern play, you see, and they saw something like it in the book where the play is.'

Beth said, 'This is Mr. Adam Harcourt, nephew of the late Maurice Unwin, and I'm his nurse.'

'Well, so you say, and I know two such people exist, but how do I know you are those people?' she said, so Beth and Adam wasted further time finding driving licences and other means of identification. At last they went upstairs.

'Mind you, I thought it belonged to my brother. You know, left him by the old man,' Evans's sister said. 'The old chap always said he'd leave Ted something but he never did, after all those years of faithful service. Service! I always told Ted he was a fool to slave his life away instead of getting a well-paid job in a factory or the supermarket.'

With that thought she threw open the door of the room at the end of the top passage. They saw her jaw drop. There was a table, the top of which was conspicuously empty, with a dust mark where something had been standing. 'Well, it was there! It's gone! It's those kids of mine!' she stormed.

To Beth it was just another nightmare; she had come through others lately and she was suddenly rather tired. But Adam wasn't tired. He provided transport and the three went to the school where the dress rehearsal was taking place. Ted's sister, wrathful because of a broken promise through no fault of her own, stormed straight into the hall where the young actors were having a dress rehearsal, and Beth and Adam pulled up sharply and watched. The cabinet was being held by two of the children—tenderly they were lifting it towards a box on which it was to be put. 'Here is the treasure chest!' one shrill voice piped up. 'I have come through many dangers to bring it!'

'And you'll come through a few more before I've done with you, Jim!' Evans's sister stormed at her young son. 'Put it down at once!'

It was evidently heavy for the children. The other child was not hers and he was evidently well aware of how Jim's mother reacted. He let go of his end and Jim couldn't retain his own hold. The cabinet fell to the ground with a crash.

It was very old and couldn't stand such treatment. Its sides seemed to cave outwards and the contents spilled in all directions.

'Gold!' the children breathed in awe. Well, certainly coins of some sort, Beth thought, and an envelope with handwriting on it, which was really all they had come for.

★   ★   ★

Beth looked across the room at Adam's mother in something approaching ecstacy. All she could think of was that it was all over, and that Adam's mother didn't dislike her.

Adam's mother liked Beth very much. She would have been quite thrilled with her as a daughter-in-law in the ordinary way but as one who had ousted Coraleen from her son's affections, Adam's mother felt she had a bonus given to her.

Never had her son looked like that at Coraleen. Never had Coraleen looked like that at her son. Every so often Beth and Adam looked at each other, during the conversations, during mealtimes, as if a magnet drew eyes to eyes, and they couldn't look away. But after a week, she was beginning to get used to it, and the young people did take themselves out a lot. Beth was just the sort of girl to help Adam crew his boat; enthusiastic, willing, unlikely to make a fuss if she got dirt on her face or the boom knocked her into the sea. Her hair stood on end most of the time, but those eyes of hers enchanted everyone, and her glorious smile was, as Adam's mother put it, (on the telephone to his grandmother) quite contagious. She herself felt like going round the house smiling all the time.

'And you say that this girl and Adam have jointly inherited this big estate of Maurice's? Well, why couldn't Maurice have made a straightforward Will in the first place?' Maurice had been only a distant relation, and one they didn't, as a noisy and happy and open sort of family, really understand. The fact that Adam had called Maurice 'uncle' had not drawn the two families together, nor the fact that Maurice had always referred to Adam as his only nephew. Nobody could get really close to Maurice. Except perhaps Beth.

'Maurice never did anything straightforward. But he certainly seems to have been taken by his little nurse. I'm not surprised—I'm taken by her myself, and I'm so delighted that Adam has fallen in love with such a nice girl.'

'Yes, but what about this adoption

business? Have they found out who her parents were?' Trust the grandmother to want that explained, even if it was a long distance call.

'Yes, I was coming to that. They had put a private enquiry agent in because Coraleen kept insinuating things about Beth. Pure jealousy and envy, I'm sure, but they discovered this awful family Beth thought was hers, and then discovered Beth wasn't related to them, only adopted.'

'Yes, but did they discover why, and who her parents were?'

'Yes, I'm coming to that! They were all in a train that crashed, and Beth's parents were killed, and this Mrs. Whiterod, who seems big-hearted even if impossible otherwise, took this poor baby because it was crying so, and she sort of kept it until the search for relatives went on, and finally agreed to adopt it when none were found. But Beth's father was a doctor and her mother had been a nurse.'

'Why didn't they discover that at the time?'

'They did soon afterwards, but for reasons of her own, Mrs. Whiterod never let Beth know. Then apparently she thought when Beth wanted to be a nurse that it might be a regular source of income for them, the rest of the family being a bit shaky on keeping a job and paying up.'

'What a dreadful person!'

'Well, no, just her type, I suppose. And I

should think that when Beth began to interest old Maurice, one can't blame Mrs. Whiterod for thinking she was on to a good thing. All the same, I'm glad things turned out as they did.'

'Yes, well, this cabinet everyone talks about?'

'Oh, that! That was most interesting. A pity it got broken, but Adam found a craftsman who thought he'd like a chance to try and put it together again. Wasn't it a strange story?'

'Uncomfortably strange. I wish Maurice hadn't been so fantastic about the way he left his worldly goods. I'm old-fashioned enough to think Maurice should have left something to such a faithful servant as that Ted Evans, too.'

'He did! In a queer sort of way, of course. I forgot to tell you. You remember when the cabinet was dropped and broke and things fell out of it? There were all sorts of things in there, and in the letter providing for Beth and Adam to inherit Staddlecombe, old Maurice said that anything else found in the cabinet was for Ted, who had so faithfully guarded the secret lock.'

The grandmother clicked her tongue in disgust at such a way of doing things. 'Well, that's something! Those old coins, I suppose!'

'Old coins! It was a complete collection, which they think will fetch quite a sum. But as there was also a pair of valuable cuff links and a fob watch in a case, Ted doesn't want to sell the coin collection. He wants to lend it for exhibition when the public start going in to see Staddlecombe. Isn't that nice?'

The grandmother sniffed again at the thought of old Maurice and his devious plans. 'Silly man, if that letter hadn't been found, the whole place might well have fallen into the wrong hands! Oh, what am I doing wasting time on the telephone like this. I must go and pack.'

'Pack? Where are you going?'

'To visit you, of course, and see this child. I can't wait. This Beth sounds a little love.'

'She is a little love,' Adam's mother said happily.

Adam felt he would never stop thinking that. He kept looking at her from under lowered lids, as he polished the brass rails. The boat was tied up in a small bay further down the coast. The sun was warm for the time of the year and the sea calm. He asked her at last: 'Happy, Beth?'

Beth had been lying on her back, eyes half closed, watching him. 'M'm, yes, of course,' she murmured.

'In spite of only just hearing about your real parents?' he persisted.

'Perhaps because of that,' she said, after a pause. 'I might never have known. As it is, it's nice to think I've unknowingly gone

225

happily into their own profession, the world of hospital. Funny, that, but inevitable, I suppose.'

'What about your own name?'

'I've been thinking about that, too. I'd like to use it but is it worth it? I mean, everybody knows me as Beth Kennington at the hospital, and if I continue my training . . .'

'Will you want to go back to the Farmansworth General?' he asked, and he didn't have to remind her of the unhappy memories there, and Mrs. Whiterod's family.

'Yes, I think I will. I don't like the idea of changing training, mid-stream. Anyway, Matron might want me to use Harcourt as it's to be my married name.'

'Still, I think it does matter, terribly, Beth. "Elizabeth Layne". It's a nice name, it really belongs to you, and it will be on the marriage certificate and invitations. Yes, I think you must, Beth,' so she agreed.

'What about Staddlecombe? Do you want to live there, Beth?'

'I've been thinking about that, too. I love the place, you know I do, and it belongs to us jointly so it looks as if old Mr. Unwin would have been pleased to see us marrying and going there.'

'It's on the cards he had our marriage in mind,' Adam said wryly.

They laughed tenderly together as they thought of the old plotter. After all, old

Maurice had nothing else to do.

'Well, it doesn't seem quite on, a student nurse cycling to the Farmansworth General every day from a stately home, does it?'

'I don't see why not, though not very practical perhaps. The same goes for my old job. They've offered it back to me and I think I'll take it, because Oliver Mason isn't directly concerned with it, and it was a good job. I can't think why I let myself be talked into leaving it, and we shall need every bit of the money after it's been taxed to keep Staddlecombe in prime condition. We're not going to be rich. The place will eat money. You know that, don't you, Beth?'

'Yes. But don't go back there—you'll be needed here to supervise. I never wanted to be rich, just to know that one didn't have to rush around borrowing if a need for twenty pounds popped up suddenly,' she said, feeling happy she had been able to pay Grace back her six pounds at once.

'I know, love. So what do we do about a roof over our heads? Live at my mother's?'

'No, no need. I thought . . . well, what I'd *like* to do,' Beth mused, 'is to have a flat at Staddlecombe. Somewhere strictly private for us to live in, and then throw open the rest of the place to tourists. Then when they've all gone home, we can wander about the place and enjoy it alone, without keeping the rooms open for a social existence we shan't have

227

time for.'

'I was hoping you'd say that, Beth,' he said, kissing her.

Later, she said, 'We can keep Mrs. Yardley and Ted Evans but I wondered if we could take on the Imberholts too.'

Adam was horrified. 'With that child of theirs making a wreck of the place?'

'No, listen, Adam, I've been thinking of that, too. He needs a male teacher, not someone soft like Shirley. There's a very good man running the local infant school near Staddlecombe. The Imberholts could have the gate house, so the boy wouldn't get a chance to wreck anything at the big house.'

'Oh, Beth,' Adam said helplessly. 'Now I can see how that Whiterod family took advantage of you.'

'I don't think they did, really. And they weren't responsible for me liking people. I think that must have been how my own parents were. I'm glad they were in medicine too. Mr. Unwin would have approved.'

'Mr. Unwin *did* approve,' Adam said quietly. 'I was keeping this back for such a moment as this, to tell you as a surprise. Another of his famous letters has been found. He had dug up a lot of your background before he decided that you should inherit. He liked digging things up about people, and he must have been well aware that Mrs. Whiterod and her family weren't your own relatives.'

Beth sat up. 'Oh, why didn't he tell me? Well, I did rather wonder about them. And to be frank, I couldn't see them fitting into Staddlecombe!'

'No, I agree. But the thing is, old Maurice *could* see you fitting in there, my dear love,' Adam murmured, as he brought his lips down to hers again. 'Just as I can.'

Photoset, printed and bound in Great Britain by
REDWOOD BURN LIMITED, Trowbridge, Wiltshire